The Lion of Venice

by Mark Frutkin

Porcepic Books
an imprint of

Beach Holme Publishing
Vancouver

This book is published by Beach Holme Publishing, #226–2040 West 12th Ave., Vancouver, BC, V6J 2G2. This is a Porcepic Book.

We acknowledge the generous assistance of The Canada Council and the BC Ministry of Small Business, Tourism and Culture.

THE CANADA COUNCIL FOR THE ARTS SINCE 1957 | LE CONSEIL DES ARTS DU CANADA DEPUIS 1957

Cover Art: *The Lion of St. Mark* by Vittore Carpaccio, 1516 (4 ft. 6 3/4 in. x 12 ft.), housed in the Ducal Palace, Venice. Map of Marco Polo's route from *The Travels of Marco Polo*, translated by John Frampton, edited by N.M. Penzer (Argonaut Press, London, 1929).

Editor: Joy Gugeler
Production and Design: Teresa Bubela, Joy Gugeler

Canadian Cataloguing in Publication Data:

Frutkin, Mark, 1948-
     The lion of Venice

(A Porcepic Book)
ISBN 0-88878-378-7

     1. Polo, Marco, 1254-1323?--Fiction. I. Title.
II. Series.

PS8561.R84L56 1997   C813'.54   C97-900648-1
PR9199.3.F776L56 1997

Prologue

In the year 1298, soon after my return from the East, the Genoese threw me in prison. I shared a filthy cell with a Pisan who called himself Rusticello. He had a bad smell and a wheedling, bothersome voice.

Marco awakens on his bed of straw, the stained wall before his eyes assembling itself out of the shards of his dreams.

He sees cracks on the wall splay out like sprigs of lightning on a map, twining across a thousand leagues, ten thousand *parasang*, a hundred thousand *li*. With his finger he absently traces his journey, winding and unpredictable as birdsong.

He supposes he is lucky to be alive.

When Marco had first returned from the East, the Doge of Venice appointed him Gentleman-Commander of a galley with a hundred oar, part of a Venetian fleet that engaged the Genoese in the Greek sea. To the boom of kettle drums and cry of horns, the Venetians sailed straight into battle and prompt defeat. Marco and seven thousand others were captured, their ships towed backwards to the port of Genoa, the banners bearing their proud lions, dragging in the waves.

He had watched with the other Venetian sailors, stunned, as they landed at Genoa under a low grey sky and the despairing commander of the Venetian fleet leapt onto the quay and beat his brains out against a stone bench.

Then Marco was thrown into a prison cell. That was three days ago.

Marco rolls over. Rusticello, sitting across the room, stares at him.

1

"Dream?"

Rusticello, a scribe and poet from Pisa, arrested for an unknown crime, shares the cell. A specialist in chivalry and its lore, the Pisan had garnered a smattering of fame for his Provencal romances.

Marco gazes at Rusticello without speaking. *Who is this Pisan? Fifty unenviable years on his shoulders, his lank dirty hair an unseemly length, fat as a friar with thick soft hands to match, nails yellow, half his teeth broken or missing, long ears with fleshy lobes, tufts of hair growing from his nostrils. An obsessive mind, too, with penetrating eyes, round and small as peas. And a sour smell, as of grain fermenting. I suppose I will smell as bad soon enough.*

Already it seems to Marco he has spent a lifetime staring at the four walls, trapped with the disputatious Pisan whose insistent, grating voice has worked at him as a knife scrapes at a mussel clinging to seaside rocks.

A salt mist drifts through the square window. Marco sniffs the air— the open sea. He fills his lungs with it.

Rusticello speaks, as if the night were but a momentary pause in their conversation of the previous evening. "So you see, Marco, I myself have penned several romance tales and I can tell you this—a work already exists. It exists in eternity; we can only hope to reveal it as it coils down out of the light and into time, where all men can see it."

From his pile of straw, Marco scoffs. "All men? Even the great Khan from his gold-lined tomb? Pah! If I have learned anything, I have learned this: the uselessness of letters."

"I take note of your cynicism, but one must be willing to make the attempt. Lord God of Angels, let me write the book, Marco. A description of the world. Tell me. Look here— I have paper, quill, ink. I am ready. I listen."

Marco gazes into the brightness, stares into the empty

glyph of the window. "I never went anywhere. My journey was simply a tale that appeared before my eyes as I rode into it. And as I pushed on I passed deeper and deeper into other tales and the tales within those and tales within those. I tell you, I never went anywhere." He rubs his hand across his eyes. "So many...words. Descriptions of the world. Tell me, Rusticello, about Pisa. How is it there?"

"Much like anywhere else. Genoa. Venezia. The time passes there as it passes elsewhere. Why do you ask?"

"What does the air smell like?"

"The air? The air of Pisa? Like a swamp on a hot afternoon. But, you avoid me." He taps the quill on the blank sheet. "Let me write the book. Now. I and all the angels in heaven are listening."

Marco, silent, gazes into the window's brilliant white light.

Conception

Venice, 1254.

Niccolo, my father, was a practical man, a merchant. He used to say there is no such thing as magic. He used to say, "Do not talk about such things, people won't believe you." But I have seen it, I have experienced magic. I know it exists.

The Lion of Venice, in a pose of extravagant stillness, sniffs the air from atop his column of violet Troas granite. A bizarre, freakish animal, he is half-lion, half-mythical beast. His mouth is frozen open under a cat's nose, and his ears are almost human, though it is nothing like a lion's head. The face, white eyes of faceted chalcedony, emits a kind of demonic intelligence. And wings: unreal, towering wings. He is a rude demiurge, congeries of metals fused around a hollow core, a bound fury, a monster, a beast! His moist nostrils tremble and flare open. The winged statue readies himself to pounce.

Uncanny, impossible scents seem to quicken him into life—crushed almonds, flashes of honeysuckle, lemon, gardenia, clove, as well as the fresh, clean odor of damp earth and starched cotton, stitched by an intriguing ribbon of seaweed.

The doors of the Church of San Marco ease open on a flood of morning light. Adriana stands on the threshold looking out into the blinding square. In that moment, she notices a lustrous current of air curling in from the sea. The square is silent, no one moves. Everything everywhere is still. For a fraction of an instant, all over the city, statues awake to their reflections in the canals. They gaze at themselves, for a moment, in the motionless waters.

And then it passes. The square is stitched, cross-hatched with lines of families leaving Mass, and the statues fall back again into their strong, silent dreams.

Adriana follows her parents out the towering doors of San Marco, floating from the cool shadows into the hard sunshine illuminating the piazza. The wind flips and curls blue and gold pennants at the square's edge. The sea breeze flows over the water, holding off, for a while, the rising heat of a Venetian morning.

The impossible magic of the Mass, of transubstantiation, still worries Adriana. *How is it bread and wine can be transformed into His body and blood? How is it that certain things in the world can change into other things?* Shading her soft dark eyes, she steps further into the light and looks up.

Adriana is strangely excited, for she thinks she has seen the wings of the statue quiver. She turns and hurries to catch up to her parents, who are working their way to the middle of the square where they greet the Polos, parents of her betrothed.

The fresh morning weather of Ascension Thursday passed and Venice was becalmed in the hottest month of May anyone could remember. Heat drained from every pore of every stone in the city. The sun was barely visible through the haze draped over the lagoons. And yet the sun seemed everywhere at once: bouncing off the viscous water of the canals, flowing out of every crack and crevice in dank alleys, igniting the sweaty gold florins falling on a barrel in Adriana's father's waterfront warehouse. Grackles on roof peaks stood silenced, their beaks spread wide, mouths open. Caught fish hit the air and went slack with the heat, their eyes clouding into white. The night held no relief. The stored heat of day radiated from the stone walls of palaces and churches. Half-dead, unable to sleep, men crowded the squares through the night, dragging themselves along claustrophobic alleys and *cortes* like sluggish ghosts. The canals offered no respite. The water was the temperature of a tepid bath and smelled like the pus of swamps.

After two desperate nights of twisting and turning in bed, Adriana, on the third, falls into a deep and dreamless sleep.

The Lion, from his perch in the piazza, sees into her balcony, left wide open to admit any chance breeze, and gazes upon her white nightdress, the ringlets of black hair on her forehead soaked by her sweat. He waits and watches.

Rooted to his column on the Molo, the small square near San Marco overlooking the lagoon, his thoughts are echoed by pulses of heat-lightning on the horizon to the east, shudderings of distant thunder from the dead-still sea. In the enormous darkness, a tongue of lightning illuminates the nearby Doge's palace roof and the cobbles of the piazza. It lights up the route through alleys, along canals, across squares, illuminates a house not far from Piazza San Marco, its second-story balcony, a woman entwined in sheets of sea-weed- and anise-laden fog.

The Lion stands and stares, stunned by the depth of Adriana's fierce beauty, the dusky glow of her skin, the black shine of her hair, the curves of her limbs. He watches her breathe, gazes into the depths of her. Again, for an instant, all is still: the canals, the sea, even the stars stilled in their traces.

Of course, they blamed Niccolo, the Polo boy, once Adriana had begun to show. They didn't know when or how it had happened, but guessed that the boy must have climbed in an open window when Adriana's father was out, dragging himself through the sweltering alleys during the hot spell after Ascension Thursday. Adriana denied every accusation as, of course, she would. The Polo boy, too, insisted on his innocence.

The families consulted a priest. As he waved his right hand in the air while slipping the proffered coins into the pocket of his cassock with the other, he explained, "It happens. No one knows why; the influence of the planets likely, or some evil done long ago. The Lord Himself knows, in such a world as this. Call me again when the child is born and I will determine its state at that time. *Buon giorno* and God be praised."

The heads of both families, being merchants with practical natures, decided that a hastened marriage was the most efficacious cure for the affliction at hand and so Niccolo and Adriana, not unwillingly, for they harboured a deep affection for each other, were hurried to the altar several years earlier than planned. In due time, the child was born and was inspected by the priest. "A slight feline cast to the eyes perhaps, and something odd about the ears–a touch shriveled–but otherwise normal."

The boy was given the name of Marco, an appellation befitting a long enduring Venetian family, for Mark the Apostle was the city's patron saint and his remains had long before been translated into the Church of San Marco. And indeed, the piazza in front of the church was adorned with St. Mark's symbol, a lion.

The years passed like a single morning, afternoon and evening, the tides breathing in and out of Venice, waves

breaking and dissolving on the Lido where sometimes I walked along the beach holding my mother's hand. I was still young and ran off with my friend, Giorgio, to catch up to the parade cutting through the sunlit heart of Venice.

Marco pointed his stick, looked at Giorgio, and shrugged as the two boys watched a man running down the street shouting into the morning air, "Lorenzo Tiepolo is chosen! Lorenzo Tiepolo the new Doge!" As people came to their windows and doors, an excited murmur filled the street.

"Lorenzo Tiepolo! It is impossible!"

"I knew it would be him. Did I not tell you?"

"Are you sure?"

"Did you not hear? Lorenzo Tiepolo."

"Lorenzo Tiepolo?"

"*Si*. Lorenzo Tiepolo."

By late morning, the entire population was surging down the crowded alleys to Piazza San Marco where the new Doge, the supreme ruler of the Republic of Venice, would be celebrated. All were in a festive mood, talking and shouting and gesturing: a crowd of tailors arm in arm singing; men drinking wine; children chasing each other. Marco and Giorgio walked with their mothers, Adriana and Antonia, and Marco's Aunt Graziela who lived with the Polos. The boys would burst into short runs through the crowd only to return and then scurry off again. The women talked excitedly about preparations for the festival that always followed the election of a new Doge.

A fine, early summer breeze whipped pennants at the square's edge as Marco and Giorgio looked over the shoulders of a group of young hooligans throwing dice under the arcades. One of the gamers turned and growled, chasing the boys away. The square was brimming with peasants from the countryside as well as wealthy families with their entourage of servants and slaves. Patrician women fanned themselves as they watched from loggias high above the piazza.

The procession began, and Marco and Giorgio, slim as water weeds and slippery as eels, wormed their way to the front of the crowd.

A flourish of long silver horns sounded as the doors of the Church of San Marco swung wide and out marched, in a fog of incense, sixteen standard-bearers carrying double-pointed banners bearing the image of the winged lion. The wind coming off the lagoon whipped the flags on the square and a spontaneous cheer went through the crowd in the piazza to be joined by those from hundreds of boats crowding the lagoon. Marco and Giorgio held their ears. The lions seemed alive, leaping and flying in unison high above the voices, claiming for Venice not only the land and sea, but the sky itself.

Heralds, musicians and young pages were followed by a phalanx of squires in puffed sleeves and round hats. Canons in long robes, a boy with a crucifix and finally the Patriarch of Venice, the city's highest clergyman, ushered ceremoniously from the doors of the Church. These were pursued by three young boys, *ballotini*, bearing the Doge's pillow, his chair and his hat. And, finally the Doge himself appeared, the majestic *Serenissima*, wearing a white Phrygian cap, and an official mantle draped over his shoulders. He was an ordinary man, an old man, and his nose was too long. But Marco soon forgot his surprise when the men in the crowd doffed their round hats and bowed as the Doge passed before them. The long line of the parade snaked about the piazza as the people cheered and whooped, *"Viva San Marco!*

Viva San Marco!"

With a shout, the parade of guilds started across the piazza to present themselves to the Doge, now taking his seat in front of the palace: dyers, sailmakers, tanners, clothing makers (dressed in gold), barber-surgeons (in circlets of pearls), the *pattenori* who worked in horn or ivory, apothecaries and spicers, charcoal makers, furriers (in robes of ermine and squirrel), pepperers, perfumers, glovers and glassmakers.

As the guild of masons passed Giorgio saw his father and shouted, "Papa! Papa!" so that his father came over to the boy, lifted him up on his shoulders and continued along with the parade.

For the next week, Marco could hear the racket of the festival far into the nights and, in the mornings, when he ran out into the square to meet Giorgio, the singing and music and dancing was starting up again. The celebrants ate mountains of food, pipes and lutes echoed from every quarter, wine ran in the gutters and spilled into the canals.

Yesterday I sat by the waters of the lagoon, my feet dangling over the side and I heard behind me, half a league away, the failing breath of my mother in her sick bed. Now I eat so my chewing drowns out the rasp of her breath. I spoon more fish, more rice into my mouth because the sound of her breath makes me want to weep, to run away, to escape.

I hear also the cut of the ships at sea, the spring caravan, returning from Byzantium.

Something is happening to me. I think my mother is dying and as she does so, my hearing reaches further and further into the distance. A sudden vast silence opens up and my mother's breath, a rattle of stones, echoes into it, and I hear voices whispering from distant rooms, crows complaining on islands over the lagoons, winds gathering across the sea.

My mother always said I had ears like fungi. She would nibble on them whispering, "Ears like crushed jewels, found under the earth or brought up from the bottom of the sea."

But now sounds, surrounded by an empty silence, fall into them as a cataract pours from cliffs into the waves.

Last night I thought I heard my father's voice (how would I remember?) from some lost place across the world. He was still alive, still alive. I heard him.

"I heard him, Momma. I heard his voice. He's coming back to us, Momma."

I felt her weak hand lift mine to her cheek and she smiled at me and nodded.

My mother is dying. And my father is worlds away, trying to get back to us– and I hear it all so clearly.

Marco went to his mother's room but his aunt turned him away at the door. As he left he heard music drifting in a window at the end of the hall, from a distant church or priory, the ever diminishing strains of a choir's failing *diminuendo, rallentando, smorzando....*

The days go by in a dark dream. Then weeks. Then months. Spring washes in and passes. The summer burns on. I am forgetting.

Since long before I was born, Gesualdo was the oldest, most revered servant in our household. As a child, I would

*see him shuffling through the halls, his hair and face the
colour of ashes, his fingers frightening and thin as the bones
of finches. But his voice was a delight, a melodious flow
pouring out of him as he hummed ancient songs, his voice a
kind of mill-wheel to keep him shuffling along.*

*If the truth be told, old Gesualdo had done little in his
later years to justify his title as servant– fetching a few jugs
of water at dawn, emptying a few pails at dusk. The rest of
his day was given over to rest and tireless flirting with the
young servant girls who flitted about the enormous kitchen
where he sat on a wooden stool in a corner near the ovens.*

From his stool Gesualdo called to young Marco, in a
voice still clear, his throat like the glass reed of the glass-
blower. Ever since Marco had been old enough to understand, Gesualdo had told him stories.

Gesualdo caressed Marco's cheek. "Soon you will be a
man, Marco. How many years have you now? Twelve?"

"I have but ten. Ten I turned, two days ago."

Gesualdo waved away a middle-aged woman servant
hovering behind the boy. "I want you to have this." He
handed a small wooden box with a sliding lid to Marco.
"Take it."

The boy held the box in the palm of his left hand and
stared at it.

"*Si, si.* Open it."

He did so to reveal a palmful of rich soil, slightly damp,
the colour of Marco's dark eyes.

"Smell it. Take some between your fingers and sniff it."

Marco did as instructed, dipping his thumb and index
finger into the box, taking up a pinch of earth and bringing
it to his nostrils. A sweet, dusty, distant green perfume with
a suggestion of resin blew through him.

15

"Where did it come from, this soil?"

"I will tell you. When I was a young man, it fell upon me to climb to the top of the column holding the great winged Lion in the piazza, there to remove the soil and weeds that had accumulated over the years under the Lion's belly and about its paws. With each step my fear rose as I ascended the rickety ladder. My heart resounded in my ears like a drum— I was sure I would tumble to my death. At the foot of the ladder my master was passing the day with one of the Doge's councillors. If I had come down from the ladder without completing my task, my master would have been sorely embarrassed. *Dio mio,* he would certainly have thrashed me, or worse. I forced myself up, a step at a time, growing dizzier with each moment. My master shouted up to me to move along, asking why I climbed so slowly and calling me a laggard. I was bit by his anger and forced my legs to lift one after the other. But, in truth, I also feared that huge shadow of the beast over my head, blotting out the sun. Sweat dampened my palms, low groans escaped my throat. I slapped my forehead— and continued up. Finally, by God's grace, I reached the end of the ladder, my eyes level with the weeds at the top of the column. The beast loomed above me like a dangerous cloud. I took the small shovel from my belt and removed a layer of weeds and soil, dropping them to the piazzetta below, taking care to miss my master and his acquaintance. I breathed in the smell of earth and was calmed by it, my heart eased by the simple odour. As I slid my spade under another patch of black loam, I thought— *suolo di cielo,* the earth of heaven— it is a contradiction, no? It struck me that the soil had flown bit by bit on the wind and collected on that high place since before my father's father's time. It seemed to me that the soil belonged to the Lion himself, was a part of him, the earth under his feet. I looked out to the nearby lagoons and the shining sea– water everywhere surrounded us– while in my hand I held a bit of soil. I placed it in my pocket and later saved it in this box." Gesualdo motioned to the box in Marco's hand. "*Si*, put it away now. And keep it with you. You might need to make use of its magic."

I didn't know what he looked like, my father, as he had left on a long journey to the East when I was very young. But then he appeared, like a ghost by the well in the corte, *and I remembered. It was like looking in an ancient mirror.*

Marco walks with Aunt Graziela to the well in the courtyard. They each carry a pair of wooden buckets with rope handles. Aunt Graziela is slow-moving, with a double-chin and a quick smile. Marco watches her lower the bucket into the black of the well. He hears the distant splash and gazes down into the depths.

From behind he hears a whisper and straightens up. Across the *corte* the dazzling light of mid-afternoon surrounds a pair of gaunt, shadowy figures standing under an arched alleyway. The two men stare at him. Graziela too turns to look at the strangers. No one moves, no one speaks. The men walk forward, ghosts coming out of the past and into the light.

One of the strangers is running towards them. "Graziela!" he shouts, his arms out. "Maffeo!" she screams, as they embrace and she covers his face with kisses. Marco stands back and watches as does the other man. Finally the man takes a step forward and Graziela embraces him too. So great is her emotion, she is unable to speak. She wipes her eyes with the hem of her skirt.

"Where is Adriana?"

Marco looks up sharply. *That voice. I know that voice.* He stops looking at the man and turns to Graziela who has brought her hand to her mouth.

"You...you don't know?"

"What is it?"

Marco knows now, suddenly realizes with a shiver who this man is.

"A little over a year ago," Graziela stares at the ground, "a sickness, we don't know what it was. The priest said he had never seen anyone die so quickly."

Niccolo drops to his knees. Marco can hear the cry rising in his father's throat long before it shatters the silent square.

My father won't tell me about the magic of those lands to the East. But I can feel it oozing out the pores of his skin, can hear it echo in his head. He would rather stick to bolts of cloth and weighing pearls. But I can hear into his dreams. I can listen with the patience of stones.

Marco watches his father test a bolt of wool from a load recently arrived from Bruges. Niccolo rubs his long hands across it as if he has a secret intelligence lodged in the tips of his fingers. He is judging the wool for its lanolin content, deciding on its quality, determining its value. Niccolo is tall and thin with an aquiline face and a pronounced widow's peak. His long straight nose and slightly sad drooping eyes are lowered, looking down now at the wool in his hands.

Despite the years they have spent apart, Marco feels there is no one he knows better. He has absolute trust in this stranger, a man returned from those distant places whose names alone thrill Marco to the depths of his heart.

"Marco," his father asks without looking up. "Why do you spend so much time staring out to sea?"

"I am listening, father."

"Listening?"

"Yes— to the chimes of Cathay."

Niccolo shakes his head. "Never mind. Feel this." He holds out the bolt of wool and Marco rubs it between his fingers. "Now smell it." Marco takes in a deep draught from the wool as he has seen his father do in this warehouse many times before. "Now this one." His father holds out another bolt of cloth. "You see the difference? You understand? This one has more lanolin in it," he says pointing to the first bolt. "Don't forget. You won't forget, will you?"

I stand, staring at the sea, listening. I hear so clearly now, I am hearing beyond the present, and into the past as well. I face east and hear a voice calling to me— and from behind I hear whispering from my shadow, as if my shadow itself has been given voice.

The voice from behind strikes terror in my heart, but the voice from the East shatters softly into a tinkling of glass, and draws further away, tempting me to follow, calling to me like the sea waves washing down the strand and hissing with foam. And beyond it all I am deaf with a vast silence that never leaves me— as if I can only hear with such clarity because beneath the sounds rests a profound silence.

I hear us preparing to head East again, hear the sound of the wind, the whip of the sail, the waters flowing. If I am to travel well I must learn patience. I must learn how to listen. I must learn about death.

I knew little about death until that night at the shipyards. Since then it has never left me, not for a moment. It is my unshakable shadow, my ticking angel. Its journey an exact replica and echo of my own.

Uncle Maffeo was on his way to check out a small coastal ship he owned with Marco's father. The ship, which usually plied the Adriatic between Venice and Brindisi carrying casks of olive oil one way and loads of timber and glass the other, was undergoing winter repairs. At the last moment, Marco had asked if he could come along.

Broad-shouldered, reserved, Maffeo always appeared to be brooding. Those who didn't know him read the look in his wide face as anger, but Marco knew that as soon as someone spoke to Maffeo his face would light up in a friendly smile.

A weightless snow was falling in late afternoon on the line of empty caravelles shifting at anchor in the yards of the Arsenal. As they stepped from his uncle's gondola, poled by Tadeo, a bearded rangy servant renowned for his silence, Marco could see winter's darkness climbing out of the lagoon and settling down on them from the thick grey sky. Walking past the deserted docks, Marco and his uncle heard the sound of workmen busy inside the sheds: echoes of hammering, shouts, metal clanging on metal. They reached the fourth shed on the left and entered.

Inside the warehouse, the Polo ship stood on logs used to roll it up the ramp from the water, rippling cold and black. An acrid smoke filled the cavernous building, coming from a cauldron of pitch about twelve feet across. Inside the cauldron, the pitch bubbled, writhing and pulsing as if alive. A spidery catwalk rimmed the interior of the building, high above in the drifting dark.

Labourers dipped long-handled pots into the viscous pitch and disappeared down into the ship's hold. Others fed the fire with splits of wood. Still others leaned forward, hammering planks.

"Come with me," Uncle Maffeo says above the din.

Marco follows him up the ladder leading to the catwalk. As they move along, stopping now and then to survey the scene below, they suddenly hear angry shouts and curses from two men further along the parapet. Marco and his uncle come to a rigid halt. The men have not noticed them. Through the gloom, Marco notices a flash of metal. A moment later, one of the men is falling, the handle of a knife sticking from the side of his neck. He lands heavily in the cauldron of pitch.

Marco stares at the scene below. A labourer runs for a rope, another for a plank, but...too late. The worker sinks backwards into the seething cauldron, sending out gentle black waves as he goes down.

Uncle Maffeo hurries along the catwalk in an attempt to catch the murderer but he has vanished into the night like smoke disappearing into fog. Maffeo finds Marco and talks to the workers about the identity of the men.

A rough old greybeard steps forward. "I recognized the murderer."

"Yes?" Maffeo nods.

"One of the Doge's assassins. Roberto, our friend, must have been punished for some crime against the Republic. We don't know what it was. He never spoke of it." The other labourers nod their heads in agreement.

"The Doge's assassin? Then we can do nothing. Before the pitch cools, fish him out and take him to his family. Clean him up first."

Maffeo takes his young nephew home. Tadeo the gondolier merely shakes his head. On their return trip, Marco fears being alone with his thoughts, but dares not break his uncle's grim silence.

Several days later, Marco woke in the middle of the night scorched with fever, his throat enflamed with catarrh. All that day he struggled in a world half-dream, half-waking nightmare, his sweat caustic to the touch.

Marco's aunt treated him with odouriferous poultices and soothing words. His father watched from the doorway to the boy's room, his forehead etched with concern. A servant was sent to fetch the doctor.

The arrival of Doctor Alberi demanded attentions similar to those surrounding the entrance of a highly placed priest or bishop. After the doctor had discussed the situation with Marco's father and aunt, he took a chair by the boy's bedside. The doctor, who had studied at the famous school of medicine at Salerno (and who let this salient point slip into his conversation with Signor Polo), was a prodigious man who exhibited extreme confidence and skill. Dressed in his fine velvet robes, he would expound upon his suggested diagnosis and its proper cure. Doubt and ambiguity neither entered his mind, nor his speech.

"It is apparent the fever has been caused because he has committed a serious sin. The influence of Mars, often a culprit at this time of year is likely also to blame. What planet rules the boy's birth?"

Niccolo answered, "His planet is Mercury."

With a sandglass drawn from his bag, the doctor took the

boy's pulse and nodded. He swished about a glass beaker of urine collected earlier and stared at it importantly. Marco's aunt held her breath as she watched the glass held loosely in the large hairy hand. If a doctor dropped the urine glass, the patient would die. "Have a servant bring me a sample of the boy's stool as soon as one is available. I would like to inspect it. What has he been eating of late?"

The aunt glanced at Marco's father who nodded for her to reply. "The usual. Eel with rice yesterday eve. And rice again at the noonday meal, with a few greens."

"Hmmm. You must understand that ague is the heat from the cauldron of the stomach rising up and enflaming the liver and heart. If one eats the wrong foods, under the influence of the wrong stars, and if one has a guilty conscience, the liver will boil, thus overheating the blood. You understand, I am sure. It is most important that the humours be kept in balance.

"Listen closely now. If the fever changes from a hectic one, which it is now, to a tertian or quartan one, occurring every three or four days, you will send your servant to inform me. Tomorrow there is a new moon, whose phase might improve things, depending on the severity of the sin he has committed. In any case, if he will eat tomorrow, feed him nothing but the milk of pulverized almonds. The day after that, if there is no improvement, give him barley water mixed with honey, figs and root of licorice. I will leave some herbs you can give him as well. If after a week there is no improvement, I will bleed him to release the evil vapors and lessen the heat. We will bleed from the side opposite the scorched liver. If a week later, there is still no improvement, he will have to be trepanned– you understand? A small hole will be cut in his skull to release the pressure of the heat mounting in his brain. For the bloodletting and trepanning

I will require the assistance of the barber."

Aunt Graziela brought her hand to her mouth, her eyes wide. A grim look passed over Niccolo's face.

The doctor took Marco's hand in his. "Commend yourself to the will of God, my son, and I am sure your recovery will follow."

"One more thing," the doctor added as they were leaving the room. He looked seriously into Niccolo's thin face. "Tonight, while he sleeps, tie a red thread about his left wrist. In the morning remove it and take it to a distant tree where you will tie the thread about a branch. In this way the boy's fever will be transferred. I have no doubt that this approach is in all cases effective. Do not, and I stress, *do not* allow the boy to pass near the tree or the fever will leap from it again onto him. Do you understand?"

Signor Polo nodded. He then invited Dottore Alberi to dine with them and the physician quickly agreed.

Although the doctor's appetite was hearty, a severe look never left his face and, several times during the meal, he sent a servant to check on the boy. Meanwhile, the doctor regaled his hosts with tales of patients he had treated and the alarming array of ailments and diseases he had witnessed: lepers near Parma; diseases of the skin, the scalp, the ears; the blood-coughers; the blind; the writhings and wailings of the mad; the spastics; the scrofulous; the paralytic; the crippled. The list of diseases went on and on: St. Anthony's fire, fistula, mal des ardents, smallpox, pest.

"The varieties of Death are most intriguing." The doctor downed his wine and motioned to the servant for more. "Death itself bothers me not in the least, but the very richness, the fertility of possible means to die, is most extraordinary. Do you not agree, Signor Polo?"

Early in the morning, two days later, Marco's fever drives

him to the balcony. In the early light, he sees the distant column of the Lion of Venice latticed in a network of scaffolding, looking like a catafalque to bear and honour the dead. For the first time he realizes his city, this occluded jewel of streets and alleys and canals running with black waters turning in upon themselves, is a kind of prison whose only relief is the sea, the open waters beyond the lagoons. Returning to bed he falls into a measureless sleep.

Later, his rheumy eyes open on a flood of radiant light. He regards a scene of unfathomable and marvelous proportions. At first he does not know what to make of it, but with effort he is able to stitch together patches of shadow and light into a fantastical image.

"If this is dream," he says, "then all men sleepwalk through their days."

Straddling his bed is the Lion, its gargantuan head forced by the wall to turn aside, its tail curling high up into a corner of the ceiling like an eel caught in its pot. Straight above him, Marco sees the metal belly hatch of the beast hanging open and a brilliant light radiating from within. Marco heaves himself up and stands, peering inside the Lion to find the light's source. Placing his hand on the lip of the hatch he pulls himself up inside and gazes directly into the light. Its brilliance is painful to behold, but he can see that the Lion's eyes are the light's source. Its blank white eyes look both out on the world and in on the emptiness.

Inside the belly of the Lion, Marco runs his hand along the cold metal plate and feels the quivering of the beast's wings.

He works his way up the narrowing neck of the Lion, squeezing through the tight opening, until his head is entirely inside the Lion's head. As if donning a mask, he places his own face against the other's, aligns his eyes with the eyes of the Lion and gazes out over the city.

What he sees is Venice in its early days, an archipelago of islands, fishing boats, frail huts standing like terns in shallow water, the bountiful sea's skin stretching into the distance. Workers tend salt pans, push rollers back and forth to pack the bases of salt. Others around the *dogado*, the lagoon area, drive larch piles deep into the swamp, hundreds of thousands of posts to support stone houses, shops, churches, palaces. Men swarm everywhere with mallets and iron bars and instruments of calculation and measurement.

Shipwrights busy themselves with supplies of timber, iron and hemp to construct fleets of ships. Venetian traders set sail for far lands, their ships laden with lumber and salt and fish, as well as human cargo– pagan Angles, Saxons, Slavs and Greeks to be sold to the Saracen armies as slaves and eunuchs.

He spies a handful of Venetian merchant-adventurers stealing into Alexandria to loot the crypt of a cathedral, searching carved sarcophagi for the yellowed bones of the Apostle Mark. At last they find them and carry the sacred relics off to Venice where they are "translated," with appropriate ceremony and vaulted pride, into the Church of San Marco.

He notices a man he takes to be a member of the physicians' guild, walking next to a narrow canal in a determined fashion. The man is covered from head to toe in an outlandish costume, like a reveler at a masque. He wears a smooth linen gown, a waxed face-mask, a flat black hat with wide brim, glass spectacles, and a foot-long curved bird-beak over his nose. This last is stuffed with herbs and drugs as antidotes against infection and the stench of the dead. The physician stops at the peak of an arched stone bridge to watch a gondola floating past, stacked six deep with corpses crawling with rats. The boat drifts down the narrow canal on its own. On the Grand Canal and across the lagoon, hundreds of gondolas and other boats, also filled with corpses, drift about aimlessly. A long wail can be heard coming from the deep wells of the city's alleys.

Out of the sea-fog Marco sees a thousand ships of Venice return from the East with entire charnel-fields of sacred relics: the bones, hair, teeth and dried bloodied rags of holy men from the Levant, from Crete, from Cyprus; knuckle-bones, femurs, skin and tufts of hair to be mounted in gold monstrances, displayed like the war-booty of holy barbarians; the ear of St. Paul, the roasted flesh of St. Lawrence, St. George's arm; a wine jar from the miracle at Cana; the whispering skull of St. Cyprian.

A man with a death's-head sigil marked on his forehead shadows his father down an alley.

He wants to scream out to warn his father but cannot, nor can he remove his gaze from the darkening city.

Marco awakens. Jumping out of bed, he hurries to the balcony to check the pillar. The Lion is there, but the scaffolding is gone. The fever has broken.

I love this city. I love its danger. I love its stench. It is a museum of death and decay. I love its patches of half-dried blood. I love it even more now that I know I am leaving– for the purple skies of Byzantium.

After winding through a maze of streets behind the Church of San Marco, Marco and Niccolo enter a great hall ablaze with light from dozens of smoky fish oil lamps, torches and thick tallow candles. In his long velvet coat and floppy velvet hat, Niccolo gazes about with a composure born of familiarity. Marco, standing close to him, regards the scene with excitement and alarm. Hundreds of men down flagons of wine and shout at the tops of their voices, in heated argument or carousing song. A group of German merchants shout, pounding the wooden table with their fists. The room resounds with the speech of Milanese, Greeks (some from Crete), and Serbians (from Zara and Ragusa). The groups of foreigners keep to themselves, knowing they are forbidden to discuss trade outside the great *fondacos* set aside for that purpose. Venetians of all classes and stripes shout and raise their jugs together. Marco's eye is caught by two dark-skinned Turks, who refrain from drink, conferring in soft conspiratorial whispers, their bulbous, onion-domed turbans touching as they incline their heads toward each other. He couldn't take his eyes off them, marvelling at their strange dress, wondering what they were saying to each other. Even with the noise of the crowded hall, he could easily distinguish their voices, intertwining in dialogue like delicate chimes of glass.

"Marco! Marco!" His father pulls him through the crowd. They stop at a table filled with faces Marco recognizes. His father's friends clap and stamp in unison by way of greeting. Father and son sit down next to each other on the bench, joining easily in the conversation.

Marco looks up as a space is cleared in the middle of the hall for a juggler and two dwarf tumblers, whose limbs seemed permanently entwined. When the dwarves roll about the room, Marco is unable to distinguish whose limbs were whose–it appears to be a single double-headed eight-limbed beast. The performance ends and the entertainers unravel from each other, tumbling into the thick crowd and disappearing. An enormously tall, thin negro walks to the edge of the open space, holding up a cask of wine at arm's length. He begins gulping its stiff red stream. As he drinks and drinks, drooling a thread of wine from the corner of his mouth and down his chin, the crowd claps and chants. Finishing the barrel, he falls to his knees and smashes the cask on the flagstones. The crowd laughs and cheers. Next comes a grotesquely fat man, his stomach hanging down to his knees as he raises his cloak and dances about, revelling in his obesity. The crowd shouts and throws coins.

The night wears on as drinkers fall under the tables and others stumble into the night. A vicious knife-fight between two old men is quickly halted, the combatants disarmed, three rosettes of blood on the flagstones at their feet. Marco falls asleep with his head on the table while Niccolo drinks and talks.

As Niccolo and Marco walk through the maze of alleys, arms across each other's shoulders, toward their own *corte* of San Giovanni Grisostomo, a voice close behind shocks them: "Stop! Do not turn around. Listen closely, Signor Polo." Marco, with his head slightly turned, glimpses the flicker of a blade and notes a mask. "I come as a friend but on pain of death you must not see me. I bear an important message, so listen closely. A certain enemy is planning to accuse you of crimes against the Republic. You must leave Venice at once."

"I have done nothing. Who accuses me?"

"You know that must remain a secret. You have made enemies. If you remain, you might well hang between the columns of the Lion and the Saint. You have a few days, but do not hesitate." Marco turns and catches a ripple of cape as the messenger slides behind a column and disappears.

The next morning, a youth comes to the door of Ca'Polo and whispers in the ear of Marco's father. Niccolo hurries out and Marco follows, unseen. When they come to Piazza San Marco, they see a small crowd gazing at the latest victim of the Doge's purge hanging upside down on the Molo from a rope strung between the columns of St. Theodore and the Lion. The man's throat is slit, his intestines curl down, and blood is caking on the cobbles in the sun. Niccolo walks briskly from the piazza while Marco lingers, frozen in the shadows, staring.

"Marco, next week the spring caravan of ships heads east. Maffeo and I must leave with it."

"And I. I too must leave." Marco could see his father trying to decide.

"No. Not yet."

"If not now, when? Please, father."

Niccolo hesitated. "Stand up before me."

Marco drew himself up before his father and righted his shoulders– no longer a boy, not yet a man.

He looked into his father's eyes. "If not now, when?"

Niccolo smiled. "Yes, if not now, when."

Marco beamed. "Where will we go, father?"

"Byzantium. There is a large community of Venetians there. We should be safe. Come along now. Many preparations await us."

I walk across the Piazza San Marco to the Molo by the lagoon, taking care not to walk between the columns of the

Lion and St. Theodore. Between them I see cobbles coated with blood. A mangy orange cat sits there licking at it.

In the pre-dawn light I hear terrifying screams from inside the Doge's palace. They are old screams still trying to escape its warren of rooms, mingling with fresh cries from victims snatched from their beds moments before. A bilious taste rises in my throat.

I turn to the lagoon where the water is crossed with bands of yellow and pink. I hear a wind starting thousands of leagues behind me– it is already upon me, pushing from behind. I hear it throwing waves onto the shores of Byzantium where the sky is purple, scarlet, amethyst, where the rain falls in drops of gold, where desiccated saints' bodies float like clouds in the cupolas of the basilicas, where a million voices chant in wondrous elegiac harmonies, their breath sighing through hanging gardens of glass.

A Jail Cell In Genoa (I)

Our failure to defeat the Genoese fleet has landed me in this damnable jail cell where Rusticello, dedicated and persistent as a maggot, thinks he will eat his way through to my dreams. But I have learned not only the delight to be found in listening, but the necessity for silence.

Rusticello places the bottle of ink before him on the upper left-hand corner of the slab of wood, pauses, his gaze held by the bottle, then shifts it a half-inch further to the left of the parchment. The thick glass inkpot is stoppered with a cork, its bottom singed. He removes the cork and places it on the slab before leaning forward to stab the ink with his quill.

"No, no, no– it wasn't like that at all, not at all." Marco sits on his straw, forearms on knees. "It was a journey of revelations, a journey in which the names of those cities and lands rang on my ears with an indescribable strangeness– Soncara, Timochain, Vokhan, Kain-du, Zai-tun.

"We had no maps. Do you know what that means? We lived on the edge of the unknown– and I, a young man, grew into that unknown. How can I hope to relocate that tale? All would be lost in the telling because I know, I know what comes next...and that's *not* how it was." Marco pauses to scratch at a flea.

Rusticello stops writing and looks up. "Yes?"

"The manuscript must repeat that journey, in its essence, and the essence of that journey was the unknown. Impossible. I tell you, it is impossible. The manuscript must be something new, illuminated from within–not a remembered map, a retracing of steps, a kind of stupidity embellished with lies and exaggerations...impossible...impossible I tell you!" His voice rises at the end as his shoulders arch forward, his head drooping. Leaping to his feet, Marco snatches the paper Rusticello holds, tears it to shreds and shoves the pieces into Rusticello's mouth. Rusticello lets him do this, watching in resigned silence and only turning his head in slight resistance when the Venetian grabs his chin with one hand and forces the bits of paper between his lips. When Marco is finished, Rusticello looks away and spits the glob out onto the floor. He stands then and, with care, places the quill and jar of ink on a high stone shelf.

"Look, you make my hair turn grey." Rusticello stands before a cloudy metal mirror on the wall in their common cell. "Marco, my hair goes grey waiting for you to speak. I will be an old man before the bird flies from your mouth. Let it go, my stubborn friend. My hand will dance to your tune– but you must speak."

Marco is thin-faced, his eyes on close inspection reveal a slight almond-shape, almost feline. Though his hair, eyes and eyebrows are a rich black, his skin is pale, yet worn with wind and weather. His hands, oddly delicate, are heavily-lined in the palms. His nose is medium-sized and straight, his lips set in such a way that a close observer might see that his teeth are clenched–with stubbornness or determination, or a combination of the two– at the back of his mouth. Somewhat taller than average, wide in the chest but thin in the hips, he carries himself in an upright manner, his eyes always seeming to look into the distance.

Marco turned, his words directed to the back of the other's head. "No one is listening."

"I am listening."

"You? You are nothing but an old man, half-deaf."

"Still, I am listening."

"No one will believe. The few who hear will scoff, call it superstition, blasphemy, lies. Who will there be to recognize the truth?"

"The truth, the truth?" Rusticello turned from the mirror to face Marco. "Who decides what is the truth? Speak to me, Venetian. You have the words in your head, I have the words in my hand— together we will make them last."

Marco sighed. "I can see the moon out the window like a slice of melon and I hear the bells of Genoese churches. The people of the East believe there is a rabbit in the moon, they too have bells. And waterclocks. And cities that rise and fall with time. But don't waste your effort writing it down, scribe. You will end by dulling the point of my sword. I refuse to speculate on the meaning of my dreams. I would rather keep dreaming, riding and counting the leagues."

Rusticello shuffled to his pile of straw. "There could be wide interest in certain dreams. I know you have seen things other men have not even imagined. You have told me, at times, teased me with half-revealed details. I have heard you mumbling half-coherently in your sleep. I listen with the sharpened ears of an old widow, much time on her hands, gossip her bread and wine, but I understand little— and when you wake you bite your tongue. Speak now, give it up, I am listening."

Marco spoke as if to himself: "It was all a dream— I myself a dream figure, moving through lands I dreamt. It was a kind of fever-dream from...."

"You avoid me with your maddening non-sequiturs. Look—it is dark outside our window. I have wasted another day trying to land that fish of a tongue. Perhaps it is useless, perhaps I should let it continue to swim freely in that empty sea inside your head."

"What?" Marco turned to stare blankly at Rusticello.

Rusticello sat brooding.

From his side of the cell, Marco muttered, "The light has gone. The room is dark but the black at the window, the perfect square window, is an altogether deeper black. It is like a dream within a dream, this perfect void of black, a perfect geometric talisman, a deep dream deep within a dream, unattainable, unrealizable, like the past within the present...that's what he told me...."

Rusticello perked up his ears, raised himself up on one elbow.

"That's what he told me...watch...."

Sucking in his breath, Rusticello listened hard...waited...then flopped onto his back, realizing Marco had fallen asleep in mid-sentence.

The next morning, sitting on his pile of straw, knees raised, feet flat on the floor, Marco said, "In any case, it matters not. I am sure my family will soon buy my freedom. I will not have enough time here to relate half the tale. Also," Marco stood and walked to the window, his back to Rusticello, "to tell the truth, I can no longer be sure what I saw with my own eyes, what was told to me in a tale, and what I dreamt in my imagination." He turned around and faced the Pisan.

Rusticello held a bowl of broth cupped in his hands. He gazed into it, at the few floating threads of meat, as he spoke. "Yes, the past fades...my own, too. But still, you saw much of magic, much of wonder, I am convinced of that."

"How is that? What convinces you?" Marco moved to the door as Rusticello set aside the bowl and stood, walking to the window to look out.

Rusticello turned to stare at Marco. "Something about

your look, your face, your eyes. One cannot look upon the wonders you have looked upon and not have one's eyes reflect it."

Marco crossed in front of Rusticello and went to the mirror. He gazed into the reflection of his own eyes. "I see nothing."

Rusticello ignored him and moved to the door, turning and looking at the floor. "Eight steps," he said and walked back to the window as Marco crossed to his straw. Rusticello looked out the window. "Yes, you have seen magic, grand vistas of land and sea, vast panoramas, mountains, deserts, great cities, and lost villages at the end of the world." He turned from the window and looked at Marco. "I can see it in the intensity of your gaze, those dark pools clear as melted ice. Oh, it's not in your grey-speckled ragged beard, not in your weathered skin, not in your surprisingly delicate hands. No, it's in those eyes, Marco Polo. There is a distance in them as of far-off places. I can see it there, still there, as if you are always looking beyond." Rusticello returned to his side of the cell, squatted and picked up his bowl. "They say the eyes are like wells– all that you throw into them stays there, and can surface at a later time. I am a patient man. Be silent if you must. I will wait."

Marco glanced up, his look hard and clear. "Remember that. Remember what you have said."

Silk Roads East of the Known World

Across the sleepy lagoon, I see tall umbrella palms on the island where my friend, Giorgio, studies at the Franciscan monastery. As my sandolo cleaves the smooth water, I hardly suspect I will not see him again for two score years– and then under quite different, less pleasant, circumstances.

From an early age Giorgio had longed to be a priest. He had entered a monastery on the island of San Francesco del Deserto, not far across the lagoons. Marco rowed his sleek *sandolo* out to see him one grey morning.

The island exuded a green-scented silence. Although a fetid mist lay over the lagoons, the warmth of spring thickened the air. The two friends walked about the grounds talking, then sat on a stone bench overlooking the walled garden edged by towering cypresses and umbrella palms. No breeze stirred. All was still and quiet, but for the odd bird twittering in the bushes.

In his right hand Giorgio held a scroll. "I have found the Papal Bull I mentioned to you, issued by Pope Alexander IV in 1260. You should heed its warning, Marco. You should stay here, learn to pray, like St. Francis."

"Yes, yes. What does it say?" Marco, familiar and impatient with Giorgio's pieties, glanced at the parchment in his friend's hands.

"I will read." Giorgio, who had a round head, stubby white hands and a delicately weak mouth, ceremoniously announced the title– "Clamat in Auribus"– and went on to read from the document, struggling over the Latin.

"And what does it mean?" Marco folded his arms over his chest.

"It says the Tartars are inhuman."

"Where? Translate it to me."

Giorgio translated, haltingly: *There rings in the ears of all, and rouses to a...vigilant alertness those who are not...confused...by mental torpor, a terrible trumpet of dire fore-warning which...giving...evidence of events, proclaims with an unmistakable sound the wars of universal destruction. Thus the scourge of Heaven's wrath in the hands of the inhuman Tartars, erupting as it were from the secret...confines of Hell, oppresses and crushes the earth....*

"Enough." Marco held up his hand. "My father says it is not true, as does my uncle. They say the Tartars are men like us. Not saints, certainly. Not even Christians. But much like the people of Venice."

"Are you not afraid, Marco? It is no sin to admit you are afraid."

"I am not afraid. I will follow my father. You can stay here and pray for us."

"I will."

They shared a piece of bread and spoke for a long while of other things. As the sound of plainchant drifted out of the nearby church, Marco, with a heavy heart, rowed back across the lagoon. He turned to look again at his friend who stood on the shore until Giorgio's still figure was lost in the mist.

I am a sailor. All Venetians are sailors. Our blood is thick with salt. I know better than most that sound travels easily over water. Tales drift to me on the wind and those same tales, same winds, drive my ship on its way.

In preparation for their voyage east, Marco helped Niccolo and Maffeo oversee the loading of goods on the ships, and watched the hiring of crews from the early morning crowds of sailors who gathered near the twin columns on the Molo, the small square by the lagoon.

After passing inspection for overloading in the San Marco Basin, the round ship on which Marco was to spend the next month joined the sea-going caravan of narrow tarettes and bireme galleys, their rows of oars sweeping smoothly through the waves.

Late in the morning under an open blue sky, the ships passed from the harbour along the deepest channel in the lagoon and out into open sea, lion pennants whipping in the brisk sea breeze. Marco thought that in all his seventeen years he had never seen anything so beautiful. He gazed back at the city of Venice disappearing on the horizon, fading like a few dusky lines on old parchment.

Two days out from the port of Rhodes Marco stood staring at the late-morning sea, the wind stretching the sails taut, a chop of waves scudding under high wisps of cloud and blue sky. Next to him leaned old Silvio, the ship's scribe, who had spent more years of his life in the Levant than in his home port of Venice. Marco broke the silence with a question that had been dogging him.

"Tell me, scribe, who is the Dominican friar travelling with us? He has spoken hardly a word since we left Venice. And when he looks at me, he seems to have anger in his eyes. Why should he be angry at me?"

The Dominican mendicant had never mentioned his purpose or his destination. Hardly spoke at all in fact. *He doesn't look like a brother, Marco had thought, not with his stubble of beard and the black circles under his hard eyes.*

And then there are his hands.

Most mendicants that he knew had soft white hands. At worst, those who spent time in gardens might have a thread of dirt under the fingernails. But not this one– his hands were like gnarled roots, the backs covered in black stiff hair, the fingernails broken. The friar seemed the embodiment of lean toughness, his wrists, protruding from the cassock, were shockingly thin, making his hands appear huge. His face was gaunt, pointed, sharp, like leather stretched over the sticks of his cheekbones. Everything about him made Marco shiver. The friar would pace the ship in a restless fever, unable to rest for more than a moment, like a dog with worms.

Silvio, his lips dry and cracked, hair white with salt, looked about the deck, leaned close to Marco and whispered, "Beware of him. He is subtle, but dangerous. Beware the moment you step from this ship."

I hear the voice of the scribe, Silvio, telling the shipmates a tale, a tale of the whispering skull of Cos. He heard the story from a sailor, who heard it from another whose father went with a Greek priest of the order of Lamanites to a cave on the isle of Cos. Inside the cave was a tiny church and inside the tabernacle of the church was a skull. It was said that the skull was that of a hermit, a saint who had not eaten for forty years and who, while still living, was borne like a feather up to Paradise. A few mendicants in nearby caves had claimed they heard his skull whispering of all it had seen in Heaven and beyond.

Silvio himself had been to the island to search for the

cave, without success, although he had found the skulls of two anchorites.

Later, in the complete blackness of night at sea I listen to the creaking silence of the ship. My ears gather in the world, drinking in thousands of leagues of night. At the far edge, like dawn breathing, I hear, I am sure of it, the whispering skull of Cos. I am mad with joy and light. I long to explode into the dust of stars, to empty myself into the long tailing winds. Instead I float in the silence and tell no one.

It was a quiet month at sea, with little sound but the dulcet wind in the sails and the forlorn cry of gulls. After stops at two smaller Venetian colonies in the eastern Mediterranean they sailed to the crowded port of Byzantium, where their ship threaded through the multitude of exotic craft that plied the waters of the Bosphorous. Domes and minarets shone on the hills of the city and sent a thrill through Marco.

Niccolo and Maffeo oversaw the unloading of goods and supplies: Flemish wool from the fairs of Champagne; linen from Switzerland; caskets heavy with silver and copper from German mines. Marco headed off, determined to follow the friar.

He had no trouble trailing the mendicant through the contorted alleys and crowded streets in the wharf area. In the large black cloak and hood of a Dominican, he stuck out. The friar stopped to purchase a hunk of bread, which he gnawed as he stopped to speak to a man standing next to an enormous cauldron. Nearby were piles of white bones and skulls. By boiling the flesh off the bodies of Crusaders killed in the battles of the Holy Land, the bones could be shipped home to France and Italy for burial in a less unsanitary way. Marco raised his arm and held his sleeve over his nose. The Dominican started moving again.

Eventually the friar entered an area that felt more like home. Venetian merchants and families could be seen everywhere, the air rang with the Italian tongue. An old man on the street pointed in response to the friar's question, and then as a wooden-wheeled cart passed laden with straw, the friar jumped unseen on its back. One of the rules of the Dominican order, Marco knew, was to travel by foot only. No Dominican would ride on a cart, especially not in a public place. Marco had no trouble keeping up, the cart lumbering along at a sleepy pace. When the cart turned into a wider thoroughfare, the friar jumped off. He entered a warren of dusty workshops, where twisted alleys splayed off in all directions. The friar stopped again to ask the way of a woman who pointed down a nearby alley with the green-topped cluster of onions she held in her hand.

Marco could hear the sound of metal on metal nearby. A smithy, the hammer falling as regular as a church bell tolls the hour. Other workshops they passed stood empty, and few people were to be seen in the streets. The friar hurried as he closed on his destination. They entered a shadowed lane with no exit. Marco had to take greater care not to be seen, hiding in doorways, behind carts. Finally the Dominican stood at the alley's end, hesitated, turned around, looked back the way he had come, and slipped through the black shadow of a doorway before him.

Marco crept to a window cut in the wall near the door. Inside, a glassmaking works contained a large domed furnace at the center with two smaller furnaces beyond it. A heap of soda ash was piled in one corner, a pile of sand beneath a large low window, firewood stacked along a back wall. Objects of coloured glass rested on shelves on a side wall: red goblets with twisted stems, sea-green vases, pink bowls

nested inside each other. Through the four mouths of the
main furnace Marco could see the fire glowing, its light shining
up into the faces of the friar and the only other person in
the room, a stocky curly-haired glassworker.

Marco listened.

"You tell me my brother wishes me to return to Venice?
And why in the name of the Lord should I do that? In Venice
I was one glassmaker among hundreds. Here I am one
among ten, and I am the richest, for I possess the secret
knowledge of Venetian glass. In Venice I could barely afford
to pay my workmen. Here I am a wealthy man."

The Dominican spoke in fits and starts, teeth clenched.
"The Doge has ordered...you know this is forbidden...this
treachery."

"I have divulged no secrets of the glassmaking art. There
is no need to worry. This place is as safe as Venice itself. The
population of Venetians here is almost equal to Venice. You
must understand. My soda ash," he pointed to the pile in the
corner, "comes from burning seaweed found in Syria, which
is not far so I save much money in shipping costs and I have
a guaranteed source of supply all year long. In Venice, when
the ships arrived late I could be left without soda ash for
months."

"The Doge has expressly forbidden any glassmakers to
leave the lagoon. *Forbidden it.* Why do you persist in flaunting
his will?"

"I admit to a feud with my brother. A bitter argument,
believe me. Rather than being faced with the necessity of
killing him, I left. You understand?"

The friar said nothing as the other turned to tend his
furnace, placing a long clear glass tube through the aperture
and bending over.

In a flash, the priest sunk a thin knife in the glassmaker's back, withdrew it, pulled his head back by the hair and in one smooth swift motion, slit his throat. Marco stood staring wide-eyed at the quick-streaming blood and, for a moment, could not move. Then he spun about and ran. The Dominican, his face vivid with reflected flames, twisted around at the scuffling sound of Marco's retreat.

As he rounds the first corner, he realizes the friar is already out the door and coming after him, his cloak flying. Marco speeds along the deserted darkening alleys, trying to remember the way back to the docks. Having more breath than the Dominican, he gains slightly. He turns left and sees a knife-edge of moon at the end of the street; turns right, and sees a half-moon over a house. He spins about. He hears footsteps behind him. *What is happening?* He turns again and finds, high above him, the moon, round and full as the pupil of an eye. Another street, another turn, and there is no moon at all. He finds himself standing in a cramped square that has five streets leading off it. He stops, his heart pounding in his ears, the breath going in and out of him like a bellows. He swallows dryly, turns around. *Which one? Which one?!* About to choose the last street on the right, he sees a flicker of shadow down the alley on his left.

The shadow clarifies into the face of the Lion staring back at him, its white eyes opalescent and empty. The Lion is so still it seems as if the entire world has come to a halt. Marco cannot take his eyes from the face of the beast. It stares at him with a look of penetrating silence that throws all sounds into high relief. Nothing moves. Marco can hear with absolute clarity, the footsteps still coming but with a vast silence between each one. A distant bell sounds. A woman coughs. A beetle scratches at the base of a wall. The

Lion turns and lumbers down the alley. Marco glances back, then follows. The Lion has disappeared, but Marco finds that the alley leads him to the docks.

Marco told all that he had seen (except the part about the Lion) to his father and uncle.

"The arm of Venetian power has a long reach. We will not stay long in Byzantium," said Niccolo.

Maffeo nodded. "Two days to sell our goods, and then we are gone, yes?"

"Yes, we shall soon leave for Acre, the Lord God willing."

Before we leave Constantinople, I spend a day watching my father and uncle haggling over jewels in the covered bazaar. The market, like a city unto itself, with its myriad of twisting roiling streets, is a cauldron of sounds. I listen to the voices and noises that fill the covered souk and don't know which way to turn.

What is it I listen for now among the bright trinkets? The black thread whispers its way through the crowd....

Marco listens to the unrelenting din, the obsessive *capriccio* of merchants haranguing each other in market stalls, the clamour of carts with iron wheels racketing along alleys of mislaid cobblestones, the ringing scales of coins falling in streams on a brass plate.

A pair of mongrels yelps and tears at a piece of moldering bone. A whip cracks. An old woman croaks, laughing. Marco's father and uncle bargain with a turbaned merchant, thin as a curved knife, over a handful of green stones and violet *cabochons* from Abyssinia. Marco stands rooted to the spot, turning this way and that, the squealing dissonance surrounding him. A merchant of musical pipes sways before his stall and flutes discordantly, smiling to himself. Three screaming children dressed in rags chase a cat. In the distance a deep *thump-thump-thump* continues unabated. The din swells and rises and thunders and is multiplied and intensified by the peculiar architecture under which it is held– an entire city of winding alleys, cubby-holes, cul-de-sacs, and innumerable vendors of spices, leathers and foodstuffs, bound under a single overarching roof, a few shafts of dusty light drifting down from on high to penetrate the gloom. The cacophony echoes and re-echoes, swells and booms.

Marco has wandered off and awakens from his reverie with a start. His father is nowhere to be seen. He hears the simple, lyrical grace-note of a tangerine bird in a cage hanging outside the market stall across the alley. He whistles back, rendering a credible imitation of the warbler's trill.

With a sudden rush the sounds of the market swell into an unbearable noise. He covers his ears. He hears the black thread of footsteps walking resolutely through the gloom, their thunder pounding in his ears. He runs, stumbles, rights himself and runs again. He sees light, daylight pouring down on the entranceway of the covered *souk*. He makes for it and stands in the fresh air, breathing, as Turks stream by him on both sides. His heart is calmed. He listens hard and hears, at a great distance, the peaceful swish of the marbled waters of Venice. A moment later, his father and uncle stand next to him and they together walk to their quarters at the *funduq*.

The sky of Byzantium was not purple, nor violet, nor rose. And now we have come to Acre, the filthiest city I have ever seen. I told father I have seen him— no, that is wrong— I have heard him, here. I will never forget the terrifying sound of that friar's voice: "Merchant," he said. "Have you seen two men of Venice and a boy. They go by the name Polo. Have you seen them?"

The merchant did not reply so I could only guess that he shook his head. But it will not be long before the friar comes to the funduq, *inquiring about us.*

"The Doge's assassins are relentless. We must go on to Jerusalem without delay. There we must gather some of the sacred oil from the Lamp of the Holy Sepulchre, a gift for the Khan," said Niccolo, turning toward Marco.

"The Khan? We will be going on then, to Cathay?"

"Yes, we must. Our only hope is to lose the assassin in the wastes of the Silk Route. He will have much less power in the land of the Khan. Perhaps he will not follow and will choose instead to await our return. I will tell Maffeo. We must leave shortly."

Onto the Silk Road at last. I fear my journey has become a kind of trial, a test. I feel as if I am struggling to give birth to something. I know not what.

The party of fifteen snaked down from the high plateau.

Marco, Niccolo, Maffeo and Rashid, the young Arab guide, on stout asses in the lead; the others– Arabs, Turks, Saracens and Persians– driving the camels following in a line behind. The Bactrian camels, weighted down with leather bags of foodstuffs and goods for trading, were sturdy and sure-footed. Fully laden, they could travel about five *parasang* a day. For this reason, the *caravanserai* where the party often spent the nights were roughly five *parasang* apart for much of the length of the Silk Route. While the land the caravan had passed through during the previous days had been dry, it was not completely lacking in vegetation. The odd tree dotted the landscape. Low brush was scattered in the hollows. Small animals darted out from behind rocky outcroppings. Above all, lizards, in a dizzying variety of sorts and sizes, had provided the party with their fill for the previous three nights. The Arabs had shown a consummate skill in capturing them.

As they left the high plateau behind Marco could see, stretching below, the beginnings of a trackless desert without flora or fauna of any sort. Darkness descended quickly over the desert and Marco called ahead to his father, "Will we camp?"

"Yes," Niccolo replied, without turning around.

They decided to set camp on the desert's verge. As the drivers unloaded tents and provisions, Rashid sniffed the air expectantly. Despite his youth his dark face bore a riot of wrinkles beneath the hood of his white burnoose. Gathering the cloak around him he made for his donkey, calling for Marco to come with him.

Riding hard, they follow the bottom edge of the cliff where it joins the meandering line of the desert. After riding a short while, Marco notices a glimmer, a mist of green in the distance. They approach a patch of trees and vegetation where a trickle of stream etches down the cliff face and blurs into a muddy pool. Half in the water and half out lies the body of a dead lion, the back legs and tail of a large lizard sticking out of its mouth. The lion's eyes are frozen open, its mouth stretched taut and wide. The Arab leaps down from his donkey and kicks the lion in the side. A cloud of flies buzzes up. He kicks the lizard's tail. Nothing happens.

He turns to Marco and points to the skins both their asses carry. Marco knows he is to fill the skins with water. Meanwhile, Rashid begins hacking the haunches off the lion to take back for meat. As Marco fills the skins, he gazes into the lion's strangely familiar face.

"Hurry, the dark comes," says Rashid, and they are off.

That night, after the meat had been roasted over coals and eaten, Marco falls into a well of sleep, at the bottom of which waits a dream. At first he dreams that he is floating down through water, down into the depths, his body slowly revolving and dropping at the same time. As he lies on his back he can see sunlight filtering down from the surface, circles of golden light, intersecting and moving in and out of one another, long bars of light constructed of myriad shifting rings. He realizes he is floating in the radiant spaces of the Church of San Marco, drifting up among the complex nested bowls of domes, cupolas, recesses, fonts, arcades, with their levels and layers, his body aswirl in the light of the gold glittering tesserae of the church's mosaics. He sees the bearded face of the apostle Mark speaking to him in Greek. The face of the saint dissolves and reappears in a coffin carried by two acolytes, followed by others in solemn procession. The saint sits up in his coffin, raises his hand as if to bestow a blessing. Suddenly a roar rises from him and he is instantly transformed, his mouth growing ever larger and darker. Marco is drawn into the mouth, his head sucked down into the constriction of the throat where he can feel the neck muscles tightening and loosening around his skull, his legs kick out behind. He is swallowed right up to the waist, the moist darkness squeezing in on him, his lungs too constricted to allow breath enough to scream. He weeps and gurgles, choking as his heart pounds at his temples and a tremendous heat drives up through the middle of his head, until at last he awakens to the dawn. He lies in a pool of sweat and stares at the bright, violent sky.

After packing up the beasts and stuffing a few dates and hard bread into their mouths, the travellers move off into the desert.

In a dusty caravanserai *east of the known world, I begin to realize that sky and stars alone remain the same. We move from one unknown to another. All that matters to us now is food and weather, and putting distance between ourselves and the assassin.*

The donkeys and camels of another long caravan approached them over a low, dry hill. Marco shouted from his camel, "Fursat bashad!" (May it be an opportunity!), and the reply came back, "Khuda bi-shuma fursat dihad!" (May God give you opportunity!). Rashid echoed, "Oghur bashad!" (May it be luck!) and the caraven driver returned, "Oghur-i-shuma bi-khayr bad!" (May your luck be good!).

For a short while they stopped and stood about under the hot sun, inquiring about the road ahead, answering questions about the road behind.

Later, a six-days' march from the nearest town, the caravan of camels and asses snaked across a stony, grey plain sprinkled with dusty camel-thorn. Marco gazed at two lines of low, black hills on each side which seemed to come together in the distance. The sky glimmered pearl grey with dull light in the late afternoon. Soon they would arrive at a *caravansarai*– the Persian guides had assured them it was ahead.

Like two ends of the same tough rope, Niccolo and Maffeo bobbed ahead of him. His father, outgoing and friendly, a slyness in his ready smile, drew out the intentions of whomever he met. His uncle would look on in silence, a silent anchor, giving wild men in wild places something to think about. One so friendly and garrulous, the other distant and pensive. It kept strangers guessing, and that hesitation, that slight confusion, Niccolo and Maffeo knew, was a useful tool. Though they were tough as leather on bone, they had their surface refinements, like weeds in the lagoon that sprout a leathery flower on the surface but have a stem that runs on and on. They were far tougher, more experienced, stronger physically than him, while Marco, with only a thread of their toughness but a more nimble mind, shared both their blood and their name.

The *caravansarai* came into view– a low flat-roofed mud-brick building. As they approached, a pair of mongrels came out snarling, to protect the donkey carcass they were scavenging. After realizing their dinner was safe, they went back to their feast, raising a small dust storm of flies.

Once Niccolo and Maffeo were assured that the camels and donkeys were hobbled for the night, they all entered the building to meet a handful of other travellers and locate a place on the floor, which was covered in straw, to lie down to sleep.

A young trader greeted them. His wizened father stood behind him and glared. He whispered to his son who directed a question to Rashid, "Who are these men? What is their religion?" The old man looked even more displeased when Niccolo, who understood the questions and disliked the old fellow's staring, answered with a traditional response in Persian, "Ustur dhahabaka, wa dhihabaka, wa madh-habak." (Conceal thy gold, thy destination and thy creed).

Later, Marco met a boy, as young as himself, on the roof of the building.

"Praise be to Allah!" the dark-skinned boy said in greeting, as he nodded to Marco and Rashid and smiled. "Where have you come from and where are you going?"

Marco answered in halting Persian.

"From the distant west, from across the sea that washes Byzantium."

"I have heard of lands in the west. Please God, tell me how have you come and what people have you seen? What is your business here?"

"Through Turkomania, Armenia Major, Georgiania to Mosul. We are traders, but in many of these places the country people kept cattle and had little to trade, but the people of the villages produced silk and carpets. And we have passed time in the great city of Baudas, anciently called Babylon, where we have traded in silks shot with gold. Now, we are heading for Cathay." After having said little all day, Marco found the need to speak overpowering. Even though his use of the Persian tongue was far from perfect, his words spilled out in a torrent, as he told the other young man of all he had seen.

They were joined by the boy's older brother who had an intense interest in metaphysics and wished to speak of nothing else. He quickly realized Marco's lack of interest in the subject.

"I have heard the men of the west have no interest in metaphysics. Our refuge is in God," he said as he *salaamed* away.

Marco and the boy, with Rashid listening but partaking little, spoke for several hours about their journeys. The night wore on. Sleep stole over them and the stars snaked through the sky.

In the morning the Polos continued on their way— another flat rocky valley, another day of tedium and dust, another pair of lines, chains of bare black hills on the right and left that appeared to meet in the distance but never did.

I hear his footsteps behind us. I bounce along on my camel in the heat and screeching light and I listen. I hear his relentless stalking. I am astounded by his persistence, by his unswerving devotion to his task.

I ask myself, what drives him? What keeps him coming after us? Is it fear, a blind fear, as in a dog that has grown vicious with constant beatings?

And again I listen ahead and I hear the soft pads of a lion passing through sand and the trickle of glass, like frozen reeds clicking together.

Even though he comes without swerving from his purpose, without hurry and without delay, I must go on. I cannot halt or hesitate or give in. I must go on, go on.

They seldom spoke of time, seldom mentioned past or future. There was too much of it; time could only be understood in small portions– today and tomorrow, the first weeks of autumn, the green days of early spring. To speak of the time of the entire journey would destroy them, would overwhelm them with its immensity. There was only the sky and the earth and the moving on– east, always east.

During the last days of summer, the party had camped among a cluster of nettle trees in low hills. Rashid split a melon twice the size of a man's head with his curved sword. He handed half to Maffeo and the two of them sunk their faces into the helmets of fruit. Marco rode over the next hill for a better view and time alone.

Marco sits on a rise overlooking a sloping hillside. A young, dark-skinned shepherdess herds goats among the lush arak trees. She wears a double necklace of coloured stones and her lips are dark crimson. The fruits hang heavy, shaking on the trees as the goats suckle from them. She too raises her mouth to one and nibbles at its tip, pulling her cloak tighter about her.

Suddenly, two men appear from behind the trees, their worn weather-burdened faces unfriendly. They have long curved knives hanging from their cloth belts. As the men start up the hill toward Marco, he turns, runs to his camel and mounts.

He urges the camel into a swift trot and then a full sure-footed run. Her shanks are stretched out in full-gallop. With his whip of twisted hide, he smacks the mountain of flesh pulsing under him, again and again. The fleet camel swims down a sandy ravine, ears pricked and tense, heart pounding. The long curved neck is erect and stiff, the head solid as a smooth stone, the eyes bulging under long lashes. The camel snorts through her dilated nostrils, steaming heat as she pounds across the earth. Marco rides her harder still. Her cheeks are smooth, nose delicate and moist, the split in her lip perfectly straight, the corners of her eyes white with pus from the inescapable motes. Under her chin, red bristles shiver as she runs, as the firm flesh of her back carries Marco through the air. With a tremendous thirst he drinks in the wind. It is as if the patchy-haired beast, the pile of skin and bone and meat is an extension of him, something alive that rides to his whim.

In turning to glance back, Marco does not notice the branch. The beast charges on and he is left to walk back to the encampment, chastened and sore.

If I were to disappear into a fable, could the Doge's assassin follow me there? It is a question I ask myself without the least irony. I am disappearing into a tale. I know it now; I recognize it, the tale opening up before me. In the city of Kierman, a carpet-maker seems to weave together the mountains and streams ahead.

Within a month, the party had arrived in the city of Kierman. There, Marco and Rashid met a blind man on the street who, when he heard their strange tongues, insisted on taking the foreigners to see the famous carpet-maker of Kierman.

The blind man bowed deeply to the travelers, then led them down an alley where half-a-dozen slim, dark boys played a game in the dirt with walnuts. The boys stood and stared wide-eyed as the strangers passed. Marco and Rashid, a stringy dog sniffing at their heels, glanced into doorways where they saw women, children and old men bent over looms. At the alley's end they entered a low building. In the soft half-light, a turbaned man with a straggly beard, intently tied knots in the carpet on which he sat. He intoned softly when the blind man greeted him, but did not look up from his work.

Marco noticed his hands, his long, lithe fingers. They moved with precision and speed but remained utterly relaxed. At times, as Marco watched, he was unsure whether the hands moved at all. It seemed as if the complex knots were tying themselves. The man held a shallow bowl of clear water in his lap and looked into it every few moments.

A boy servant brought in tea for the guests on a large tray of hammered copper. The carpet-maker did not stop his quiet work.

"From where have you come, travellers?" he asked without looking up.

Marco proceeded to tell him of their travels. The carpet-maker nodded and kept working. When Marco stopped, he said, "Go on, please, tell me more of what you have seen and where you have been. Tell me everything. I have great interest in the wide world and yet have travelled little." So it was that Marco went on in detail about his journey.

Hours later Marco said, "And so it was that our party– Rashid and I, and my father and uncle, and the others, as well as many heavily laden camels and donkeys– arrived in Kierman yesterday morning."

The sun had begun to set and a cool wind swirled into the room. The carpet-maker kept at his work. "Allah be praised. A fascinating tale and you tell it well. Allow me to give you the gift of a tale as well." He glanced at the bowl in his lap.

The boy served more tea and the carpet-maker began,

his hands continuing to tie knots, his fingers as if moving through supple currents of water.

"There once was a carpet-maker renowned throughout the lands of Persia. His fame had even spread as far as Baghdad. This carpet-maker was famous for rugs of astonishing beauty and workmanship. He would work into his rugs the stories he heard and events he witnessed. It soon became a great honour to appear in one of his carpets. When the Caliph of Baghdad heard of these wonders, he had the carpet-maker brought from his village to the city and appointed him his *ustad*, or master designer. There the Caliph bid the carpet-maker make rugs that told the story of the Caliph, to his great and deserving honour. This the carpet-maker was happy to do, choosing not only to design the carpets but to work on the rugs himself, revealing the life of the Caliph in his knots. And for many years he served the Caliph with honour and distinction."

Marco, as he listened, gazed about the room. The carpet swept down from the vertical loom, filled the entire floor and ran on into another adjoining room which was dark. Marco could not tell how large the other room was, but sensed that the carpet somehow filled that room as well and ran on yet again through a further doorway which he believed he could discern in the distance.

When Marco had first entered the main workroom and looked at the carpet it seemed alive, shimmering with activity and life. Its intensity had overwhelmed him, drawn him in like a whirlpool or the sea's breaking wave, where all is motion and change and swirling knots of froth. After his eyes and mind had grown calm, he had gazed at the carpet beneath him. Parts of it were fantastically rich with geometric decorations in complex patterns. Other parts swirled with arabesques, palmettes, toothed wheels, crab-like *harshangs*, cartouches, rosettes and eight-pointed stars. The carpet was a fertile teeming world: lions, hyenas, elephants, horses, dragons and other beasts both real and mythical; cities peopled with craftsmen, scholars, soldiers and pilgrims; shimmering s-shaped streams and glades of cypresses and willows, and distant silver mountains; archers on horseback riding through a birch forest; gold and crystal palaces, and great mosques. Marco heard the swish of a fountain in the courtyard and the sounds of a young man singing *ghazals* which blended with the wind's breath through the carpet's orchard of almond trees. Marco followed the blue meandering line of a stream that passed under the trees and was led back to the carpet-maker's fingers tying knots of water.

He watched closely as the rug-maker, his knots like details of Arabic writing, returned to his story.

"The Caliph was proud of his carpet-maker and showed the magnificent works to all visitors who passed through his lands. Many years passed like a single morning, afternoon and evening. One day at the beginning of the season of lemons, the carpet-maker displayed a rug to his master that brought a questioning look to the Caliph's face. "What is this? What have you done here, my good artisan? I do not recognize these scenes. These are not scenes from my life." The carpet-maker himself had no explanation but returned to his work in a cloud of confusion. But as surely as the sun clears the mist from the fields of dawn, so was his confusion clarified. As he worked in his doorway the next day he watched the Caliph unknowingly perform the actions the carpet-maker had predicted in the carpet.

"One day soon after, the carpet-maker realized he had knotted his own image walking into the mountains and, by the next morning, guards reported to the Caliph that the carpet-maker was gone. The Caliph sent his swiftest horsemen in all directions but he was not to be found."

Rashid and Marco thanked the carpet-maker for his story, finished their tea, and looked out at the night, sheets of black at the windows, and a fine silver rain beginning to fall.

Marco took a sip of tea, then pointed to the carpet. "How is it you have found such a rich yellow for these sunflowers?"

"For the sunflowers, I dyed the thread with saffron crocus." The rug-maker spoke without looking at the sunflowers.

"And the red flowers in the tree?" Rashid pointed.

"The dye for them was produced with the dried bodies of female cochineal insects. I employed cherry juice for the cardinal singing near the top, and madder for the earth underneath."

The servant came to clear the empty tea cups. The blind man stood and bowed, telling Marco and Rashid that it was time to go. As Marco thanked the carpet-maker for his tale and his hospitality, he noticed details of his own journey appearing in the rug and, under the carpet-maker's hands blossomed the fields, deserts, rivers and mountains further east, the ones Marco would traverse the next day and the day after that. Glancing quickly back the trail they had come along, Marco spotted what he was looking for– a man in a dark rain cape sitting on a black horse, following them.

At the door, Marco hesitated and looked back. Rashid, already outside, waited in the dark. "One more question? Why do you keep a bowl of water in your lap? I have noticed that you glance into it every few moments?"

Without looking up, the carpet-maker replied. "It is a reminder."

"A reminder? Of what?"

"That even as I tie these knots of mountain and stream, there is another much like me, on the other side, untying them one by one."

With that, Marco nodded and stepped out into the night.

I know now the assassin can follow me into the tale itself, as if he were my double, my reflection in dark water.

From within his dream, Marco heard a spark *snap* from the guttering fire, then *ping* off metal, bright shiny steel. He rolled quickly out of his blanket and into the fire even as the sword came whistling clearly through air and sliced the hairs from the side of his head. The dulled fire had life enough in its coals to shock a scream out of him, waking the others and chasing the figure back into the night.

Rashid applied herbs to the back of Marco's burned right hand.

"Who was it?" asked Niccolo. "Could you see?"

"No. I saw nothing, but I hear him even now riding three leagues to the south, cleaving the still air with his curses."

Niccolo gave his son a puzzled look. "It could have been anyone. A bandit. A robber."

"It was the Doge's man– the assassin."

"How do you know this?"

"His curses are Venetian. I recognize them."

"This is the worst of luck. He continues to follow, even here. The Lord protect us."

There exist dangers other than the Doge's assassin– but whenever there is danger he is near.

The party continued its relentless push to the East. Within a week, the caravan entered another desert, a nameless waste that Rashid did not recall passing through on his previous journeys. But the local guide insisted and Rashid said to trust him, so they followed. They passed no one and saw nothing save for the odd, whitened bone or the dried, leathery carcass of a donkey or a goat, sticking half-out of the sand. Marco wondered that the local guide and the camel drivers could find their way through the confusing terrain of sand dunes and rock outcroppings.

In late morning, when the wind from the east began to rise, blowing sand and dust into their faces, Rashid leapt from his lead donkey and quickly roped together the camels and asses so they made a single long line stretching across the desert, while Marco raised his cloak to the level of his eyes and prepared to face the storm.

"We must keep moving through the sandstorm or we will be buried," Rashid shouted to Marco as he tied a rope from the tail of his father's donkey to the neck of Marco's.

The wind gathered and swirled, sand and dust blinding the men and animals, the air thick, the sky blotted out. Marco could feel his stout donkey drawn along by the tugging rope as they stuttered into the wind. In the midst of a furious gust he was toppled. One moment Marco was on the back of the animal, the next he lay on the ground. Already the sand was burying him. Leaping to his feet and crying out, he groped about trying to find the caravan. His words died an arm's length from their source and his mouth filled with dust and sand. He stopped. The sand climbed to his knees. He edged forward, blinded, struggling against the wind, his face wrapped tightly in his cloak, shrouded like a walking corpse. Every few moments he would peek out. There was nothing to see but swirling sand.

He heard music, cymbals and drums, and the clash of arms, men shouting and crying out and he grieved for his father and uncle. He heard his own name being called by a voice that did not seem to be of this world. With great fervour, his lips and tongue bone-dry with fear, he repeated over and over, "Lord God of angels, preserve me."

After a while he felt the wind drop. Lowering the cloak, he glanced out and saw that he stood in a space where the wind had calmed. He could see the sky above and yet whirlwinds of dust encircled him. Astounded, he watched as a band of brigands waving curved swords and riding on asses passed out of the dry fog at the edge of the open clearing and back into the storm. They had not seen him. Then the winds again engulfed him and he slipped back under his cloak.

Hours later, the wind again dies down. Marco stops his aimless walk. This time when he opens his eyes he is prepared to see the storm, as before, raging in the distance, for he can still hear its fury. Instead, standing in the clear space before him, staring at him, is a panting, full-grown male lion. The wild, heavy-lidded, yellowish eyes of the beast are riveted on him. Marco stands stock still. The heavy smell of the beast thickens the air. He can feel his heart pounding hard in the side of his neck. He is unable to avoid an involuntary intake of breath as the beast edges forward, preparing to pounce. Its long black-tipped tail twitches back and forth. The lion snarls, showing its gleaming teeth and dripping tongue which has soaked the bottom part of its mane. A sudden movement causes Marco to look to his left.

The winged Lion is there, staring at Marco. Although the storm rages nearby, in their clearing all is stillness and silence. Marco hears distant shouts, hears drops of saliva drip from the lion's tongue.

Suddenly seeming to sense a presence at once of its own kind and not, the lion flicks its tail and flees. Then the storm swirls and all goes dark.

The wind dies a third time. Marco hears its roar moving further and further into the distance. Cautiously he lowers the cloak. A half-league away stands the train of camels and asses. His father and Rashid have spotted Marco and are riding hard toward him.

I listen but there is nothing. And I learn, every day I learn anew, that listening hard to the echo of nothing can be a salvation.

Weeks, months, years– what does it matter and who can keep track? The days go by, in any case, uncounted, forgotten, fading into the dusty background of desert sunrises and mountain sunsets, disappearing into long afternoons hard with brightness, and shimmering nights.

Each day looks the same. Another road, another cloudy-eyed face, another clangourous, stormy market. I imagine we are travelling in circles– passing through the same towns and villages, over the same low rise in the distance, through the same endless desert. It is maddening– the Silk Road goes in a circle, a circle that grows ever tighter. We are not riding off to the edge of the world but coming, inexorably, to its centre.

I grow intimate with the horizon, though it keeps its distance. It moves no further away– but neither does it come closer. And what will intervene between here and the horizon– gullies we cannot see, a long flat plateau without trees, mountains that appear out of the blinding light? We ride on and on and no one passes us and we pass nothing. By late afternoon we have not drawn a single step closer to the horizon that circles us round. We are a caravan caught in sand.

Last night the jackals barked and wailed, mocking our loneliness, mocking the pitiful defense of our fire. Have we not passed this same dry leafless tree over and over again in the past three days?

We will ride forever.

Finally, we come to a stream. I can see the pebbles at its bottom like birds' eggs under clear water. The stream runs on and disappears, a ribbon of light twisting into the distance. From this angle it seems to disappear in the pool of the sky. In a moment we have filled our leather bags with water, cross the stream and ride on.

No one speaks. There is nothing to say. We are like monastics on a religious pilgrimage, our thoughts pared down to each footstep. The clop of hooves. The tinkle of a bell around a goat's neck. The wind. But no one speaks. The vastness of the world has entered us, taken us over.

The party had ridden up out of the hot wastelands and was negotiating a high mountain defile, a narrow passage between stone cliffs no wider than a pair of donkeys. The breath of the riders, of the horses and donkeys, could be seen dissolving into the cool thin air. For three days they had not passed another soul, had not seen anything green, not even a patch of dry lichen on a rock.

"Watch our guide closely." Rashid leaned toward Marco and pointed ahead. "Through this high pass, he never hesitates, despite the fact he knows not the way."

"He knows not the way? Then how does he pretend to

guide us?"

"He moves from one skeleton to another, from this thicket of bones to the next, for the miserable pack animals that have perished along this way mark out our path. It is our way. We move from one small death to another, and on and on."

Marco cocked his head at a distant sound. "Wait." His eyes stared blankly at the sky as he listened.

"What is it?" Rashid searched his face.

"I hear a bowstring being drawn, and fearful breathing. We must turn back."

Kicking his donkey into a trot, he hurried ahead to his father and uncle. "Father! We must find another way– I sense a danger in this passage."

Niccolo pulled his donkey up short. "What is it? I hear nothing."

"Nor I," said Maffeo.

"Believe me, father. There is danger ahead. We must turn around."

"Let us speak to the guides."

After a brief discussion with the two Persian guides, the caravan was turned about and headed back the way it had come. As it left the defile, a terrible wail echoed from deep inside the cut.

The guides took them on a trail that went higher into the mountains. The sky turned to a muddy purple bruise and snow began to sift down, at first slowly, then more and more thickly. The wind sharpened and they stopped to don heavy animal-skin coats and woolen hats.

"We must find shelter," Niccolo shouted over the wind.

The guide spoke. "Nearby there is a cave, but the snow comes too fast and covers the trail."

Marco looked at his father. "We must wait here. I can

find the cave if there is a pause in the wind."

They waited, the snow already halfway up the donkeys' legs. As soon as the roar of the wind abated a moment, Marco shouted with all his strength into the rare air. Then he listened, his mouth half-open.

He pointed to the left. "This way," and he urged his donkey into motion, the others following.

In a few moments they sighted the mouth of the cave and made for it.

As the drivers herded the pack animals, dusk rose from the darkening valleys.

"What did you do when you cried out?" Rashid asked.

"I listened to my own shout and heard the hollow echo of the cave. In that way I chose the direction."

Rashid shook his head. "Allah is with us."

I come to the edge of the world as we know it.

The fever attacked Marco first. It came upon him after the evening meal of wild hare by the fire, and by midnight he was rolling around in his blankets under the stars, raving, disjunct phrases boiling out of him in a torrent. A polyglot of Arabic, Persian and Italian spilled from his mouth, his eyes torn wide, unable to recognize Niccolo or Maffeo. Rashid wiped Marco's brow with a cloth soaked with water, but he thrashed about on the ground, screaming and foaming at the mouth. Niccolo grabbed him then for fear he would roll himself under the feet of the nervous, shifting camels. This brought a semblance of calm to Marco and he fell asleep in his father's arms.

By afternoon of the next day the fever had struck Niccolo and Maffeo, and in early evening Rashid too began to fall prey to severe retching. No one in the party of travellers escaped, although Rashid's case was a minor one, leaving him capable of bringing water and succour to the others. Scattered among the tall trees men lay on the ground and groaned, calling in weak voices for blankets or water.

Marco gazed up through the leaves at the empty sky. The patches between the shimmering leaves were not blue but white. A prayer fell half-formed, half-remembered from his lips. Prayer seemed suddenly irrelevant or unnecessary or too much effort. He sensed that his father lay nearby. Raising himself on his elbow, he glanced to his left and saw him, not ten paces away, lying on a blanket, his mouth and eyes open wide, his lips cracked and grey.

The sound of horses woke him from a fitful sleep. He had felt them coming, three horses, from a long way off, their hooves echoing up through the earth. He heard Rashid talking, the voices of three men as they questioned the Arab. They were moving among the trees, surveying the bodies lying there. With effort he rolled onto his back, stiff with terror that the face he would see staring down at him would be that of the friar-assassin. Instead, a man with almond-shaped eyes and unblemished cinnamon-coloured skin smiled and said something Marco did not understand. Behind the round bald head, a green warbler began its evening chant high in the tree.

When Marco awoke, an idolator monk was rubbing him down with an oily mixture containing odourous camphor. Marco asked for water, was given a cup and drank his fill. Rashid, sitting nearby, explained that the horsemen had taken them to a monastery in the foothills near where they had camped. The sprawling building was filled with Tibetan monks of all ages. The bald-headed monk, holding forth a cup, silently urged Marco to drink some tea. Marco sipped at the tea and turned to Rashid, who sat on the floor next to him.

"My father and uncle? Are they...?"

"Yes. They are very ill but improving. These monks have their herbs and their magic."

"And you?"

"I am ill, but not too much."

"How long will we be here?"

"This no one knows. You must rest a long while. Our travels have been difficult; they have sapped your strength. But you are strong and young– you will recover." Rashid took a cup of tea from the silent monk.

"How far are we from the Khan's city? We are within his realms, are we not? To have come so far and not be able to go on and finish the journey, it is...."

"Calm yourself. Yes, we have come far. We are on the edge of the Khan's empire and we could be to his capital in two, maybe three months. But it is impossible for now."

Marco gazed about the room. A simple cubicle with a single window, at one end a low table littered with small statues of their idols and what appeared to be lamp wicks floating in butter. The floor was of flat stones set in packed earth. He slipped into a slow-moving river of sleep.

Have we lost the assassin? Has he given up and returned to his black master in Venice? I fear these thoughts almost as much as the demon himself– they are careless thoughts, thoughts of the soon-dead.

Marco roamed in and out of the land of fever, a wanderer in dreams, a traveller in mists. He woke and saw Rashid near him, a look of concern etched on his face.

"Is it morning or eve?" Marco asked, but by the time the answer came back he was gone again, wandering the valleys of his fitful sleep.

By late summer, Marco was able to take solid nourishment, a small bowl of *tsampa*, a bit of pheasant or antelope. A week later he could spend a half-hour sitting on the stone terrace, looking over its low wall at the distant mountains, before the fatigue invaded. Another month and he was capable of walking for an hour in the low hills, an old monk by his side fingering a string of beads.

One morning Niccolo came to his room. "Winter soon will come. They say there is much snow in this region." Niccolo, with his fine long head, stood by the high window, gazing out. "We must go to the city of Campichu, one day's travel from here, and spend the winter there until we can continue our journey in the spring."

"The spring! That will be almost one full year from when the fever struck!"

"This cannot be helped."

"But the Khan– is he not awaiting your return?"

"I fear he has long ago despaired of our return. In any case, you mustn't travel any great distance yet. In Campichu, you can begin to learn the language of Cathay, as well as that of the Tartars. When the snow melts, we will leave for Karakoran."

Marco turned toward the wall and spoke quietly. "Do you ever miss Venice, father? Do you ever think of returning home?"

Niccolo gazed down at his son. "No. I have put it out of my mind. There is no turning around, not now. Like all

Venice's assassins, this one will never give up. Like a dog that has clamped onto a leg, it will not let go until its skull is crushed."

A Jail Cell In Genoa (II)

This Pisan, in his own way, is as persistent as the assassin. He never lets go, seems to have but one purpose in this life. One day I may be forced to throttle him. My only refuge is silence. I will speak when I am ready to speak. When the tale is complete, then it will begin.

The candle flame wavered as Rusticello eyed Marco, his difficult companion, thin of face and form, sitting cross-legged on his straw, gazing fixedly not *out* the window, as Rusticello sensed, but *at* it, the perfect black square, compass of night, jewel of nothingness.

Without altering his concentration, Marco spoke. "Am I mad, that I find immense pleasure in the perfection of the window's shape? The square, the square into which all other shapes fit; a form befitting emptiness, a nest of space, the bit of peace it provides me."

Rusticello, on one elbow, said, "It faces east. Venice. Your home."

"And beyond." Marco looked about the cell. "And here we wait, inside this perfect cube."

"Three nights now I have heard you cry out in your sleep."

"Yes, what of it?"

"You cry 'Maria, Anna. Maria, Anna.' It rends my heart to hear you."

"My wife and daughter." Marco bowed his head and stared at the floor. "My father is old but has great wealth. He will soon buy my freedom. I am sure of it."

"The roads between here and Venice are slow. Such negotiations are delicate and can take a long time."

Marco again stared at the window. "Maria has lovely green eyes, and Anna, my baby, has thick curly hair. I dreamt of them again last night."

Rusticello nodded, then signaled a change in subject by sitting fully up and leaning back against the mottled stone wall. "Do you see, it does not matter whether your tale is true or not. Your dreams are just as real."

Marco turned from the window, his salt and pepper beard disheveled, his tired eyes gazing hard at Rusticello. "Why is it you always come back to the same subject? You are a dog gnawing a bone. How can you believe my tale when I myself question it, question whether it truly happened?"

Rusticello took his turn gazing out the window. "Either what you say is true, in the eyes of God, or it is the most magnificent Devil's lie ever concocted. Either way, it makes no difference." Rusticello tried prompting him. "Tell me about your fellow travellers. What were they like?"

Marco thought a moment.

"Did they have beards?"

"Yes, they had beards. And Niccolo was the taller. No, I believe Maffeo was the taller."

"Perhaps they were the same height?"

"It is possible." Grackles could be heard grumbling in the distance. Marco stood and looked into the mirror. "Niccolo had a large wart on his left hand– or perhaps the right." Marco shook his head. "No, no, I remember nothing. They are but shades now, ghosts of memory. Impossible to hold." He hardened again into silence.

Perhaps the Venetian is playing a game to ridicule me, a bit of sport to pass the time. Perhaps the Venetian never went further east than Curzola or Modon. Rusticello looked into Marco's face but could read nothing there.

"How long have we been here?" Marco stretches out and stares at the ceiling.

Rusticello sits with his back against the wall, searching his hairy arm for a flea. "I have been marking the days." He points to the wall, then peers at it. He slumps back against the cool damp stone. "And so here we rot knowing nothing of our fate. Bah! Does it matter?" Rusticello pauses and hangs his head. "God in Heaven, I am hungry. There is nothing I would not give for a joint of pork, or better yet, a roast capon."

"I, a man of action, who has travelled to the ends of the earth, further than any man alive, am now stuck in this room." Marco glances about as if seeing the four walls for the first time. "Stuck," he points down, "in this room, doomed to travel here," he points to his right temple. "Here!"

Rusticello stood with his back against the wall of their cell, arms hanging at his sides, his palms flat against the sweating stone. That morning they had awakened to find an acacia leaf on the floor of their cell. Thinking it had blown in through the window in the middle of the night, Rusticello called it an omen, telling them they would soon be free. This possibility of freedom he looked upon with mixed feelings— if it came too soon he would never have the tale from the Venetian.

Rusticello glanced about. "I sometimes believe you are the Antichrist whose arrival was prophesied last century by Joachim da Fiore in his calculated ravings." Rusticello paused, thinking, head cocked. "Perhaps it would help unstop your tongue if *I* were to tell *you* a story. I know many. Know you the tales of Chretien de Troyes? Perhaps you have heard his romances from the court of Champagne?"

Rusticello's question was met with silence.

"He claimed to have found the written source for his tale in a book in the library of Saint Peter's Cathedral in Beauvais. A lie, of course. A vain attempt to lend ecclesiastical authority to his work."

Marco remained still.

"His tale, *Cliges*, begins and ends in Constantinople, a place you tell me you have seen. Perhaps the story would interest you? No? Another, perhaps? Maybe the one titled *Erec and Enide* which begins, 'The peasant has a proverb: *What you scorn may be worth much more than you think.*' No? Then perhaps the one titled *The Knight With a Lion.*"

Rusticello was sure he had noticed the slightest possible twitch in the Venetian's neck, a stiffening, a subtle turning of the ear. He went on, gazing at the ceiling.

"Yes, I remember now. He said, 'Every lover is in prison....' I remember it. It is all coming back to me now. Would you like to hear it?"

Rusticello was shocked to see Marco turn to gaze wide-eyed at him. "Yes, tell me."

In the parchment-coloured light of an early spring evening, Marco and Rusticello both lay stretched out listening to the last birds singing in the dying sun. The warm damp rose from the earth and flowed in their window. The first star gleamed in the square of darkening blue.

"If we could remember everything we would be over-whelmed," Rusticello said to the ceiling. "The flood of faces and images would destroy us."

Marco grunted. "The past is useless. Memory is nothing more than dreaming backwards. Nothing happens in the past." Marco raised himself up on one elbow and looked at the Pisan. "Are you an alchemist?"

"I have some knowledge of the alchemical arts. Let me tell you what I have learned about the possibilities of base matter."

Flopping onto his back again Marco sighed audibly, "No. Don't."

Later, from the anonymous dark, Marco's voice came, so quietly Rusticello thought at first that the Venetian was talking to himself. "I once knew an alchemist, an Arab, our guide. He was young although his brown face had the wrinkles of an old sage, like the crackle-glaze of a dried stream. He learned about alchemy from the academy at Alexandria, through the Nestorians. He learned also from the Chinese, on his few visits there. Don't excite yourself, my friend. I am not about to divulge the tale you have long awaited. But his face appeared to me just this moment. This Arab knew about the green lion that devours the sun. A lot of good it did him, in the end. At any rate, he knew the treatises of Jabir ibn Hayan and al-Razi and Avicenna and Zosimos of Panopolis; he knew the enigmatic text called Turbus with its anagrams, allegories and myths. He knew of the eagle-lion, the dragon with the magic carbuncle in its head. I saw his face a moment ago, but it's fading away." Marco paused.

"Yes?"

Marco passed his hand over his eyes. "A curse on the Genoese. I long for my young wife, my child. I can no longer remember their faces either. Of necessity, I have put them out of my mind. Now I have your face instead. Your face to gaze at day in and day out, for weeks and months on end, its haggard beaten look, like an old sad dog. And you have mine."

The cold penetrated every stone of their cell. Cold coming up from the floor, down from the ceiling. A damp ever-present chill. Rusticello paced back and forth, a moth-gouged brown blanket wrapped tightly round him.

"Blast the faceless whoresons who put us here! It must be colder inside than out."

"Mmm," agreed Marco from his pile of straw where he lay shivering with a blanket pulled up to his chin. "At least it dulls the fleas."

The small sliding window at waist level in the thick door opened. A meaty hand with thick clouded nails pushed a steaming bowl, grey and chipped, through the opening. Rusticello bent down and took the bowl in both palms (*like a ritual of the Mass,* Marco thought), took three steps and handed it to Marco who was in the process of sitting up. He returned for his own bowl and the window slid shut.

They began slurping the soup, happy to have something to warm their innards, Marco using an "apostle" spoon, one of the few personal possessions he had been allowed to salvage from his ship. The spoon boasted a handle in the shape of the apostle Mark. It had been a gift from Marco's godfather.

Marco held the spoon in the air, halfway to his mouth, and looked into it. "What do you suppose it is? The meat, I mean."

Rusticello nodded. "Cat."

Marco did not hesitate but shoved the spoonful of soup into his mouth.

They ate in silence.

After a while Rusticello glanced up at the window. "It's snowing."

Marco looked too. Placing the bowl carefully aside, he struggled to his feet, walked to the window and stood taking deep breaths of the outside air. "Snow has a distinct smell. I love the smell of snow."

"Does it snow in Venice?"

"On occasion. It is strange. This moment, just this moment, I feel I have never been happier in my life. Is it not strange? To feel this? Here?"

Rusticello kept eating. "Cat," was all he said.

Marco, standing at the window, was mumbling to himself. He stopped and turned around.

Rusticello pointed. "Your soup. It's getting cold."

The Red Sun of Karakoran

Snow tumbles into black waters and the earth roars, all its rivers engaged and raging. The Mongolian spring begins in the open sky of the nomad. From the edge of my hearing comes a constant, undulating drone. Deep blue sky melting.

From the window Marco watched the swollen river unsnag flat chunks of ice along its reedy edge and hurry them into the flow. In moments they had disappeared. A flock of small grey and white birds flew in controlled disarray above the river, shifting with the rapidity and grace of leaves on a single branch.

The door to the room stood open. "Marco," Niccolo roused his son from his reverie. "In five days, we will be ready to leave. The year has passed quickly."

"Yes, father. Yet, I have learned that 'to journey is to wait'."

"I am glad you have had the time to learn the languages of Cathay and of the Tartars. When we see the Great Khan, you will conduct yourself with honour and will make a fine impression. I am sure of it."

Marco had grown almost as tall as his father. "I am impatient to be on our way."

"In five days," Niccolo repeated on leaving.

Marco returned to the view out the window. A stiff wind scoured the sky. A pair of mandarin ducks pumped overhead. Higher up, a small flock of bar-headed geese swept east, in the same direction as the flow of the river. The world was alive and moving, charged and ecstatic with warmth and new light. Across the river he could see a minaret above the block-like houses, arranged without pattern, like sugar crystals spilled from a bowl. He heard the distant voice of a

Mongol ululating on the stone bridge that arched over the river. A man pulling a cart passed by without slowing or looking up. Further upriver, Marco could make out three or four skin rafts pulled onto the shore, piled in haphazard fashion. One of them was draped with a fishing net. Here and there along the shoreline he could see trees with feathery green buds, and one or two blushing with a pink glow.

He thought about the day he had spent in the bazaar of Campichu a week earlier. The first warm day of spring, the merchants pratted and jabbered like grackles. Shepherds and Buddhist monks had come down from the hills, seemingly the whole town was out taking the sun and visiting in the market square. Marco heard Mongol, Chinese, Turki and Tibetan from every quarter.

He had just passed the piles of wicker cages where the animal seller kept pheasants, geese, ducks and hares. A small antelope stood tethered, soon to be sold for a wedding feast.

On an ornate perch carved of wood roosted a green and yellow parrot, pecking grains from its keeper's palm and cackling in a farrago of languages, crying out against Tangut bandits in Chinese, ululating like a Mongolian woman, swearing in Turki. The children in the crowd stood and stared, entranced.

The parrot turned toward Marco, cocked its head, trained its shiny pebble eye on him and screeched what Marco knew to be the Chinese word for "stranger." Marco was stunned and when all eyes in the crowd turned on him, he immediately left the bazaar. He felt dizzy, almost fell as he turned a corner, as if he were being chased, but there was no one. He spun about and looked up at the sky just as a shiny black raven passed overhead.

I come to the caves of the Flaming Mountains. Did I dream what I saw and heard there in the strange light, strange air?

In his year in Campichu, Marco had never stopped hearing about the Buddhist caves in the Flaming Mountains and he was determined to see them before leaving the region.

A guide had been recommended and when Marco and Rashid went to visit him to make arrangements, the old man, with a wise though innocent smile, had agreed to meet them in the morning at the first well east of the town. "You must enter the Flaming Mountains only with a guide who knows them well and who is pure of heart," he had said. "I am at your service." He smiled. Three times he had refused payment until finally Marco simply left two gold bezants on his table as they left.

The next morning, the man riding toward them on a donkey as they waited by the well was not the old man. This one was younger, tall, light-skinned, his beard patchy as the hair on a camel's haunch. He was the younger brother of the first guide as the older one had taken ill in the middle of the night and did not want to disappoint the foreigners. The man demanded payment before they set out.

The cool evening air smelled of smoke, roasting goat and the redolent frankincense gum Rashid chewed. The Uighur, with his dark eyes staring constantly at Marco, had said nothing all day. Marco decided to sleep with his knife unsheathed.

The next morning they rode toward the Flaming Mountains, their bare sinews of clay and stone glowing red in the sun. At one point they could see a cliff face scored with openings at various heights. Tying their mounts to trees, they entered a cave mouth at ground level, the guide carrying an unlit torch and a sack.

The first few rooms were well lit by sunlight coming through the openings in the cliff face and contained a few sculptures and frescos. As they walked deeper into the mountain riddled with rooms carved out of the soft stone— *it is like being inside an enormous skull,* Marco thought, *inside a stone honeycomb*– the light turned dusky. The rooms were filled with heathen statues of gods and goddesses, some voluptuous and enticing, others wild-eyed, demonic and terrifying. The walls of the rooms were completely covered in frescos of dusty pink, blue, green and yellow, depicting the stories of holy men and the fate awaiting unholy sinners. The scenes ran like rivers of colour along the sinuous walls.

The Uighur stopped and, using a flint, lit the torch. Marco felt his stomach lurch and almost stumbled.

"What is it?" Rashid's hand steadied his shoulder.

"Nothing. Nothing...I am fine."

The room was filled to bursting with wild images of hell-beings all spinning in a claustrophobic swirl, dancing with rich black shadows. And then, in a sudden hot wind, the torch flashed out, followed by a grunt from the Uighur.

"Rashid."

"Marco." The voice came back but already from a distance.

"Rashid!" Marco heard his own voice echoing up and through the honeycomb of caves.

From far off and from all directions at once he heard Rashid's voice calling back, "Marco!"

Marco heard the silence filling in with subtle, disturbing sounds. No echo of footsteps or voices, but the sounds of scurrying things that had been hidden earlier by the hiss and sputter of the torch and the sound of their own footsteps and conversation. The swish of bats sweeping the still air and rodents or blind lizards scrabbling over the dirt. In the distance Marco could see a faint light. He started moving toward it, his hands feeling the air in front of him. As he edged forward the rooms seemed to brighten into a kind of vague twilight. The statues of full-breasted goddesses began beckoning to him, seducing him. The face of a demon, its head crowned with skulls and wearing a necklace of half-rotted heads, leapt out at him.

Suddenly Marco was running, then he felt himself in space, in mid-air, and with a whip of light he fell into nothingness.

He woke face down in the dirt and turned onto his right side. His right hand and elbow shot sharp pains up to his shoulder, then ebbed into a dull ache. The room glowed with yellow light. *Sunset. The sun must be low in the sky and can penetrate further into the honeycombed mountain.* He faced a statue of a buddha that was reclining exactly as he was. *He is asleep. No. Dead.* In the silence a dream came back to him. A man holding a diamond cut in half and a book, perfumed smoke drifting from its pages with a pleasant hissing sound. Behind him was a burning house, like a house he had seen in a village where they were burning a dead man. *I must remember this dream. It is a dream of how to die.* Marco lay still and listened. Far off he could hear the whispering of the Uighur. He went stiff on noticing a second voice, struggling with the language. The assassin's voice. Then silence.

Later, he heard a shout and a while after Rashid appeared holding a torch at the door to the room.

"By the grace of Allah, you are safe. Come. The Uighur

is gone. We can return now. I have hidden the horses."

As they rode back, Rashid broke the silence. "Your assassin has his helpers now. We must take great care."

Lost oases, with clusters of pine trees and tamarinds, pale-skinned poplars and wild asses. A short stop, then driving on. A desert threaded with mountains, and loess cliffs that must be circumvented. A desert where we come to hate light and bless the darkness. A place like death. Eyes too dry to tear. Time empty of meaning. We give the camels their head, the camels who can smell a drop of water from a distance of a thousand parasang.

Everything has to be brought along on the backs of camels or asses: food, water, fuel. Every bit of camel dung is collected, caught almost before it hits the ground, as if it is brown gold. The turds are dry– after twenty days everyone is shitting dust.

The rootless and shifting desert is empty even of smell. No smells, except the smells we bring with us and those are accentuated to a measure that would drive men mad: the heavy animal smell of the beasts, the dry astringent smell of the Muslim drivers, the smell of leather and metal, the rich, meaty, almost overwhelming smell of warm water in a sheep-stomach bag.

Two days into the Taklamakan desert, the line of heavily-laden double-humped Bactrian camels struggled up a ridge of sand, their feet sinking deep with each step. At the top of the dune, Rashid pointed ahead into the distance. Marco saw the peaks of the Tien Shan range white with snow. The air was strikingly clear. Marco knew those mountains were hundreds of leagues to the north. Turning in his seat, he gazed south where he could perceive the Kun Lun mountains. A third range, the Pamirs, unseen, closed off the desert to the west.

The caravan halted and the head camel driver came stumbling back to speak with Niccolo. Three of the camels had come down with foot sores. Niccolo and Maffeo decided they would camp for the night.

That evening the drivers sewed pieces of heavy leather to the feet of the injured camels. Marco watched them as they worked on the beasts, half-a-dozen grizzled, dried-up men intent on their labour. In the dusk, Marco noticed that the drivers, usually ebullient as grackels once they had eaten, were borne down by a vacant silence. And in the morning, when the caravan tacked into its first dune, all of them, men and camels alike, seemed to move with an imponderable weight.

By early morning, Marco's mouth was dry as a camel hide and he longed for the lush juice of the tight-skinned veined grapes popular in the oases of the region. But the grapes were gone, sucked dry by an unforgiving sun.

In the distance, Marco eyes a shimmering lake of light, a white and empty eye staring straight up into the burning heavens. All day the mirage of the lake persists, the eye burning, like the terrible sun doubled, an eye that moves at the same exact pace as the caravan, staying a half-league out of reach. Marco rubs his own eyes with his cracked hands as he bobs along on his camel.

Suddenly Rashid's old camel halts, refuses to go on, sticks its mouth under the sand. Rashid hurries to tell everyone in the party to cover their noses and mouths by wrapping them in felt. The wind ticking higher, sand kicking up, soon the full fury of the storm is upon them and they are lost to each other and to the world.

The *karaburan*, the black hurricane, rubs raw any exposed skin, but passes quickly this time, and when Marco unwraps the felt from his face he sees before him a perfect reflection of themselves, another caravan stretching across the desert, half-buried in sand. As they approach, Marco realizes it is not a mirage but a line of real men and camels, utterly still, that was once buried and has now been uncovered by the furious wind. The party approaches in fearful silence. Marco dismounts, joining Rashid, his father and the others who walk in terror and amazement along the line of camels and traders all perfectly mummified by the dry desert air, the men with pinched, eyeless faces, the camels like leather stretched over sticks. Rashid reaches up to a sack draped over the back of one of the camels, pulls it down to the ground and rips open the dusty rose-patterned cloth to determine the caravan's trade. He releases a white fluttering cloud of silk moths.

After a tasteless dinner of stale bread and tough mutton, it seemed to Marco that everyone in the party drifted sadly into sleep under the pulverized quartz of the stars sparkling overhead.

Marco pulled out the tiny box of soil he kept in his pocket, the one the old servant Gesualdo had given him. Sliding it open, he saw it was dry; sniffed the now odorless soil. Working up a scruple of gummy spit, he let a stringy drop fall into the soil where he formed a dollop of mud with his index finger. He sniffed again and he held the smell with him, in his dry lungs, in his wet mouth, as he drifted into the rich swamps of his dreams.

The next morning Rashid pointed to the nostrils of the camels which grew distended, their breath quickened, their stride stretching. Soon the whole party could smell it: moist earth, the perfume of vegetation and putrid flesh, growing in intensity and richness with each hour that passed. But this was the most dangerous moment of all. Still three days more of desert. One driver ran off in the night, unable to stand another moment, determined to find his way in the dark, never to be seen again. Marco wept tearlessly in his sleep, like a dry riverbed oozing, wept with longing for release. Later, he asked Rashid to tie him to the legs of the tethered camels so he too would not run off.

Two days later they saw it. Behind a few high trees in the distance stood the castle of Karakoran, where the governor of the region had his palace. Then they came to a small river and rode in on their camels, sliding off into the delicious sparkling water.

Encamped on the edge of the town, the sky clear and riffling through layers of ever darkening blue, Marco sat with his back against a stone and watched a nearby tree stitched with bats, their sweeping flight arcing in and out of the branches, never touching the tough dried-leather leaves. He pulled his cloak tighter as a coolness rose out of the earth and a sword-tip of moon appeared over a distant hill.

Niccolo and Maffeo stood by the camels, talking with a handful of drivers. Something in the air quickened. Even the most subtle sounds trilled and beat against his eardrum— the twittering of the bats, crickets scritching, the grunts of the camels, the occasional braying of the asses. Wide awake, he listened as the moon sliced the indigo sky.

Rashid stood holding a leather bag which tinkled when he knelt in the sandy earth next to him. He removed an instrument of brass. "For measuring the stars," he said, glancing up. It reminded Marco of a similar instrument he had seen the captain of the ship use on the journey to Constantinople. The four thin disks of the astrolabe tapped together as he placed them next to a flat wooden box, a smooth stick, a sheet of parchment with what appeared to be a star-table on it and a worn leather-covered book. As he set about lighting a fire, Rashid spoke quietly.

"We will smite the sand and learn what is ahead for us." His worn brown hands worked easily at the fire-making, setting a tangle of dry sticks. Without warning, flames started up from nowhere. Rashid returned to his objects and sat on the ground next to Marco. He opened the book and read a few phrases.

"I invoke Kebikej, the *jinn* who rules the insect kingdom, to protect the book from worms. In this book I will record the result of our geomancy. But first," he set the book down, "I will smite the sand inside the *tekht reml*." With his cupped hands, he gathered sand from the ground which he deposited, in a slow stream, in the open box. He shook the box from side to side. With slow and deliberate movements he picked up the smooth stick and began making lines of random dots in the sand.

A gusty wind had picked up, blowing from the east, stretching the fire and scattering sparks. Rashid said, "We are all *gherib* in this life; strangers, exiles. We are far from home. We must defend ourselves against the unknown." He looked at the symbols he had written in the book, consulted the star chart and spoke quietly. "It will be many years before you return to Venice, my friend, but they will pass like an arrow flying from the bow."

"What will happen?"

"I will leave you soon. You will have your journey delayed a little, before you reach the Great Khan. But, be patient, he will greet you like a son."

"And my father and Maffeo?"

"They will live long, as will you, and, after many years, all will return home."

"And what of the assassin? What can you tell me of him? When we enter Cathay, will we be free of him at last?"

"I fear not. He will follow in your steps for a hundred seasons."

In Karakoran, I meet the daughter of an old Tartar warrior. Under her spell I forget, for a while, the chase and the fear, where I have come from and where I am going.

Fourteen days they spent at Karakoran. On the third, Rashid and Marco crossed the city's market-square, bustling with merchants, traders and vendors talkative and ebullient as magpies, walked past mounds of almonds and pistachio nuts, piles of oranges and dates alive with bees, to buy apricots and eggs from a beautiful dark-haired young woman who had caught Marco's eye the previous day. When Marco had asked why the eggs in her basket were dyed red, she hadn't answered him, but took one of the eggs in her long fine dusty hands and cracked it between her fingers to show that it was hard boiled, then held out the halves of red, white and crumbled yellow to Marco and Rashid. She smiled and told them her name was Duan.

She smiled again on seeing them and informed Rashid that her grandfather, Asutai, would like to meet the strangers, as he too had travelled much in his youth and would like to hear tales of the distant world. She gave them directions and they proceeded to a quarter on the city's outskirts where they found the grandfather's house adjacent to a field of apricot trees stretching down a hill. Outside the simple square brown house of unglazed mudbricks, under a sinewy grape arbor, the venerable grandfather and a friend sat on straw mats at a low table playing a game on a large chequered board. Nearby, a handful of hens scratched in the dirt, their red wattles dancing in the sun.

The two old men (the friend was a deaf-mute) stopped playing and the grandfather offered his guests flat bread and *kumiss*, fermented mare's milk. Rashid and Marco also sat on cross-hatched straw mats eating and drinking and telling of their travels, respectfully answering the slow thoughtful questions of the white-bearded grandfather who had a nest of brown wrinkles at the corners of his eyes. The old mute kept nodding at them as they spoke, as if he understood, his eyes shining like pebbles in a stream.

In answer to a question from Marco, the grandfather explained, "A game of war–the armies oppose each other as they would on the field. We two were once warriors and now we spend our days at games and memories. I will tell you what it was like. Each Tartar warrior had his fleet horse and two bows of bone and sinew. With one bow I could shoot a distance beyond the last apricot tree there; the other bow would help me defeat the strongest enemy at close range."

Asutai told them of his youth, when he rode with Temujin, Ghenghis Khan, the one born gripping a clot of blood in his fist.

"I have seen enough blood spilled to fill the rivers of the world," he said with a touch of sadness. He had a hard line to his jaw and a dead spot in the center of his left eye.

The old grandfather told of mountains of skulls at Nishapur, where they decapitated all survivors. He told of the women who came behind the riders and slit the throats of the wounded enemy on the battlefield.

As Asutai talked, he would glance up at the sky to measure the arc of the sun through the branches. When they rode for battle, each soldier was allotted four horses, regularly changing mounts, eating and sleeping in the saddle. For strength and sustenance, they would stop, slit a vein in the weakest horse and drink the blood.

"Out there," he pointed to a yurt at the edge of his field, "I will show you the dried skin and skull of my best horse, dead now forty years."

He brought out another jug of *kumiss* from the house and they drank into the late afternoon, the sun turning red as it rode beyond the distant hills. He paused and said, "And now Kublai is destroying it all, destroying the Mongols. We are a great people but perhaps we fought for nothing." A dry, bitter look had taken over his face as he gazed across the fields. "The Khan is no longer a true Tartar, but has the black heart of a Chinese dog. If I were not so old, I myself would mount my horse, ride to Cathay this moment, and slit his throat."

Marco and Rashid, uncomfortable with Asutai's half-drunken talk, were happy to see Duan walking up the road toward them. She exchanged a few words with her father, after which Asutai turned to the visitors and announced: "You will stay to eat." Leaning over, he grasped his mute friend's shoulder and shook him awake. The mute stood and walked down the road the way Duan had come.

Sitting on stools at a rough wooden table in the dusky gloom of the house, they prepared to eat the broth, lamb and bread Duan had cooked. Before they began, Marco watched closely as she took a bowl of broth and fat and went to the small shrine by the door. There a family of felt and cloth puppets was arranged–Nagatai, the god of family, crops and animals, with his wife and children. Duan's movements grew slow and deliberate, a sign to Marco that this was the start of a ritual, enacted, he supposed, at the commencement of every evening meal. Dipping two fingers into the fat in the bowl, she delicately rubbed it on the lips of the central puppet. Marco watched closely as she stroked the little god's lips, watched how her fingers and the puppet's mouth glistened.

Her slow dance enticed Nagatai, releasing the flood of his rich, moist power.

It awoke a memory in Marco. The caravan had just cleared a low hill, he and Rashid and another guide on horses in the lead. They had come upon a solitary lion feasting on a small striped roe-deer. The lion looked up in surprise, its mouth soaked in blood. The yellow eyes of the beast and Marco's eyes met and locked, for a moment. For many nights after, each time Marco closed his eyes to sleep, he would see the eyes and mouth of the lion looking at him. Eventually words began to rise from the beast but in his half-waking state, Marco could make no sense of them.

Duan walked to the open doorway and poured the libation of broth onto the ground outside as a distant muezzin's call set nearby dogs to barking. A few chickens scattered and reformed in harmony with her motions. She came back to the table and they ate.

Throughout the meal Marco could not take his eyes from Duan's mouth, with deep-set clefts at the corners. He watched closely and listened to her voice, soft, melodious and deep. Through the open door, a slice of the waxing moon appeared in the sky. He watched the moon untie itself from the branches and arc slowly across the heavens.

We have been traveling again for weeks, across the earth, under an enormous sky the colour of pearl and skin. Like the Mongol nomads of old, we are one with our horses. I never sleep so well as when I sleep on the earth under the open sky. I am never so clean as when bathed by the rain, never so refreshed as when I breathe the crisp winds of dawn. The rivers with their plentiful fish are ours, the wild trees with their small tough fruits, the sun and the moon are ours. Our words are few and simple, we are tethered by few wants. Our guides have taught me how to smell rain coming from two days off, we know the paths of animals, the cry of birds in each valley.

We come across another desert. In those vast and vacant wastes, at first one is overwhelmed by the need to believe in God. After the emptiness has penetrated to the marrow of one's bones and to the core of one's heart, it becomes impossible to believe in anything at all.

I sit now under a pine tree some distance from the others. We have stopped to make camp, but an uncanny silence is in the air. I see the winged Lion not forty paces away, staring at me. All is still. I listen.

A bell. A drum. A strong, clear bell out of heaven and the beat of a drum in the distance, a beat as steady as the earth. I hear them, not with my ears but in my chest, as if they are a sound I am remembering.

Tomorrow we enter Cathay.

A Jail Cell In Genoa (III)

Why is Rusticello here? Why has he been put here to torment me? One moment he seems like a gluttonous monk; the next, a candidate for sainthood.

A bowl of black olives. Red wine in a stoneware cup. A jug on the floor between them.

"It must be a feast day of some sort." Rusticello takes an olive between his index finger and thumb and stares at it.

"Perhaps it is *Sensa*." Marco smells the wine in the cup before taking a sip.

Rusticello glances at him. "The Venetian dialect is a mystery to me. *Sensa?*"

"Ascension Day. Today, the Doge and his retinue will take to the open waves in his golden barque, the Bucintoro. He will throw a diamond ring into the waters, once again marrying Venice to the sea."

Rusticello nods. He eats the olive with gusto, his teeth sinking into the meaty flesh, and follows it with coarse bread soaked in pale green olive oil.

Both look to the window at the sound of bells rising from nearby churches and echoing in the Ligurian hills.

A pause, while they savour their wine, and take more bread dripping with oil.

"Did you say you have spent time in my city?" Marco licked his fingertips.

"Yes." Rusticello leans back against the wall and moans. "I have eaten too quickly." He glances at the window, and holds his belly, then belches loudly. "Yes, I was there when Jacopo Contarini was Doge. The painted frescos on the outside walls of your palaces and churches left a strong impression on me. But, of all the wonders of Venice, the Church of San Marco struck me most deeply."

Rusticello lifts an olive, holds it before his mouth, takes a nibble, followed by a careful sip of wine.

He flicks the olive pit out the window. "Like Venice itself, San Marco has the feeling of an illuminated manuscript. It also has the air of a crypt. The church reminds me of a huge reliquary, a mausoleum, a jeweled calculus, its walls filled with bones. It is nothing more and nothing less than an intricate glittering casket. The most profane temple in Europe, it belongs not to the Church, but to the Doge, who, I know, has his private entrance from the Ducal Palace and his private window from which he can view the Mass. Do not misunderstand me, I do not criticize you Venetians, I only state my observations."

Marco has his eyes closed and is rubbing his temples. His teeth are gritted tight. Suddenly, he drains the dregs of his wine and flings the cup against the far wall where it shatters into pieces. He stands over Rusticello. "I want out of this damned hell-hole!"

Marco stalks to the window, looks out, returns to his pile of straw and flops drunkenly onto his back. Rusticello looks at him, then turns to gaze out the window. The bells have ceased ringing. In the newfound silence, Rusticello whispers a warning, a breath of the prophetic: "You will never leave till you let go your tale."

Some days later, Rusticello, on his pile of straw, smiled to himself and sighed. "Live eels from Lake Bolsena soaked in sweet Vernaccia wine then roasted over olive-wood coals."

"You dream like a glutton, Rusticello, yet we live here like monks."

"God's peace be with you," the Pisan gave the monkish

greeting.

"And with thy spirit," said Marco.

"Mmm." Rusticello thought a moment, his index finger over his lips. "You know, my friend, I have been thinking. There are but two great actions a man of our day can take: enter a monastery, which is, after all, a kind of prison; or go on a crusade, which is indeed a form of travel. You see, I am a man of my time, having made my pilgrimages, by the grace of God, to Rome and Jerusalem, although I have yet to don a scallop shell hat and walk the entire St. James Way to Santiago de Compostela. And you, even though you are not a religious man, Marco, you have taken part in your own way: your journeys have been your pilgrimage; your time here in prison, your forced monastic life."

"Yes, I suppose." Marco stood and paced about the room. "The world offers deserts for the mystics, monasteries for monks, and prisons for fools like us."

Rusticello sat up. "We have done much, seen much, in our time. And now we have this." He motioned to the bare walls.

They sat a long while listening to the silence, drinking it in, immersing themselves in it, resting in the emptiness. Their cell grew ever more silent with a silence that came both from outside, from the great darkness, and from deep inside themselves, from some hollow bottomless core. Night filled in the square window. Night and silence penetrated every corner of the room, every crevice of their dreams.

Out of the middle distance, out of the virgin blackness, sparkled the extravagant *arpeggios* and *glissandos* of a nightingale.

One evening Marco watches Rusticello intently as the Pisan paces back and forth mumbling to himself, saying his half-remembered Provencal poems like prayers.

Marco sits on his straw holding a bowl in front of him. Rusticello wonders what the peculiar Venetian is doing when Marco dips his fingers in the bowl and rubs fat from the stew on his lips. But Rusticello says nothing and Marco does not explain.

As if seized with a spasm, Marco leaps to his feet, hands clenched in fists at his sides. "Why are you here!? What are you doing here!? Trying to pull some secret from me, as if I have hidden a cache of jewels from the East!"

He drops to his knees and stares at the floor while Rusticello remains standing with his eyes wide, gazing at him. The Pisan turns and goes to the window. Hands gripping the cold stone sill, his back to Marco, he looks up into the darkness and speaks, as if to himself or to the night. "Why am I here? Yes, why? To tell stories, I suppose, merely trying to hold onto a tenuous thread of sanity by telling stories. I grant it's not much, but I know nothing else. I don't know how to hunt or fish or sail or soldier or tailor. I know how to tell stories, to fashion words out of nothing and spin worlds, and in this way I avoid the two deaths: death by a surfeit of living or the death of abject emptiness– the two extremes. As for secrets–I begin to fear you would not recognize them even if you did possess them, although I am sure you have your secrets as all men do. Perhaps you more than most. As for jewels, I speak not of jewels. I speak of other things."

Into the Realms of the Kublai Khan

Finally I meet the Great Khan. He is treated like a god. At our first meal together, I do as the others do, stuffing the silk napkin in my mouth while he eats so as not to contaminate his food. His audience chambers are lined with ermine and zibelline and all who enter must wear white leather slippers so as not to soil the lush carpets. He has forty-seven sons and daughters and an insatiable lust for every aspect of life, his face red and round as the Hunter's Moon. He wants to know all there is to tell about where we have been and what we have seen. On the morning after our arrival in the capital, we go with him to shoot in the Imperial gardens.

Marco raised the short Tartar bow of mountain mulberry in an arc against the sapphire blue sky, the string flickering with sunlight, and let the arrow fly.

"You are good with the bow, young Marco." Eyes smiling in his round Mongol face, the Khan tugged on his split beard as he watched the foreigner again take relaxed, careful aim at the red and yellow silk-covered target.

"Tell me more about this man you found along the road. Where was it?"

"Two mornings ago, on our final march to the capital– perhaps fifty *li* to the west. The dead man was lying in the middle of the road and had a thick jade plug jammed in his mouth."

"How odd." The Khan stroked his drooping moustache. "What do you think it means?"

"I have no idea, Your Majesty, but I did sense that the man was left as a warning to us."

"Why?"

"The way the peasants acted in the next village. As if they knew we were coming. I heard whispering."

The Khan, seeming to lose interest in the discussion, turned to Niccolo, standing nearby with Maffeo and Rashid. "So, you have failed to bring me the one hundred priests of your Pope so that I could learn of the magic of Christendom. It matters not. It is good you have returned."

Marco held out his bow as he fitted another arrow. About a bow-shot's distance to their left, shone the blue lake of the Khan's garden. The Khan gazed at it and tugged at the fleshy lobe of his right ear. Addressing Niccolo he said, "You tell me the boy has certain talents? I have already noticed his way with languages– he speaks Tartar like one of us."

"And Chinese, Tibetan and Turki as well," Niccolo added. "It appears, Your Majesty, that my son has the ability to learn a language with miraculous ease."

The Khan lowered himself onto his tiger-skin stool and nodded. "This could prove useful."

"But, My Lord, there is something else, something most unusual." Niccolo glanced at Marco who stood with the arrow fitted in the bowstring, the bow held deftly in one hand.

"Yes?"

Marco lowered his eyes. A shimmering silence rose with the light off the lake. The Khan had a passion for silence. No sounds could be heard from anywhere within the palace, no sounds could be heard from the nearby city. The Khan had banned all unnecessary noise within half a league of his court.

Marco listened. "I hear six riders entering at Eastern Gate, two laden carts leaving from Western Gate. At Northern Gate, three children chase a cat. I hear a woman entering at Southern Gate, walking back from the marshes."

"How do you know it is the marshes from which she returns?" The Khan leaned forward from his stool.

"The reeds she has picked rustle against each other as she carries them."

The Khan turned to a retainer. "Send out my palace guards to the four gates. See if this is true."

They continued shooting at the targets and, in a short while, the attendant returned out of breath. "Your Majesty, the boy speaks the truth– the guards found six riders at Eastern Gate, two laden carts at Western Gate, the children at Northern Gate and the woman who returned from the marshes."

He handed the Khan a slim green reed.

I learn that the Khan likes tricks, little jokes to make his vassals occasionally look foolish. But, no harm done. I seem to have found favour with him, in this land where the end of things is often as not the beginning.

The Khan had twenty-five of his concubines brought into the room for Marco to inspect, Mongols from the region of Ungrat, fair-skinned and young. They were not all beautiful, but Marco passed this off as an idiosyncrasy of Tartar taste in women. His Majesty insisted that Marco number them from one to twenty-five, showing how he would rank their beauty.

The first night, the Khan sent him number twenty-five instead of number one. With skin like pig leather, thinning hair and rotten teeth, she entered Marco's chamber and promptly educated him in delights he had never dreamt possible. The next night the Khan sent him number twenty-four, number twenty-three the following night, and so on, night after night, until the arrival of number one. Marco looked at her supreme, transcendent beauty, her translucent skin, her jet-black hair. He drank in her fragrant scent of roses and wild thyme. He swam in her eyes clear as the wind-swept heavens. But twenty-four straight nights of love-making had depleted his powers. He fell asleep, and woke in the morning with the *S* of her sleeping form perfectly echoing his, her breasts pressed against his shoulder blades, her open mouth in his hair.

A disturbing rumour from a peasant shatters my momentary peace of mind. I discover that the Khan's sanctuary, his paradise, is a deception. Why is it, now that I am here under the protection of the Khan, I still feel as if I am running, spiralling in further and further to a mysterious centre?

"Are you a teller of tales then?" the Khan shouted.

The pig-tailed peasant, shivering in fear, looking pitiful in his ragged clothes, knelt before the Khan and spoke to the floor. "No, Your Majesty— it is the truth. At least, the truth of what I heard. As I say, my brother, a Buddhist monk, on returning from a pilgrimage to a holy mountain in the Western regions, said he heard this from travellers there."

"Tell us what you told my officer."

"Yes, My Lord."

The Khan turned to Niccolo, Maffeo and Marco who sat to the side. "Listen closely." He looked at the peasant. "Speak."

"Yes, My Lord. My brother said that he heard there was a man from lands far to the West who had come to a village near the mountain. This man had with him a huge Tibetan dog of a reddish colour. Everyone in the village feared this vicious beast for it was half the size of a horse and could rip the belly out of a man with a single snap of its jaws. The dog was so vicious that the people of the village...."

"To the point."

"Yes, Your Majesty. The man kept the dog closed up in a room in his house for days without food or water. In the field behind the house he constructed a straw man with clothes and leather boots that looked much like the son of the merchants from the West who passed through the village some months before."

"Did the straw figure look like this man?" The Khan pointed at Marco.

The peasant looked, wide-eyed. "Yes, Your Majesty. From the description my brother gave. Yes, I think it is perhaps him, though I cannot say for sure."

"Then what happened?"

"The villagers saw the man stuff sheep offal into the shirt of the straw figure, then lead the starving dog out and let it attack the figure to get at the food. He did this many times. Over and over. The dog would tear at the straw man, ripping it apart to get at the sheep guts. Then the man and the dog left the village."

The Khan waved his hand and the peasant, half-bowing, scurried out. The Khan turned to Niccolo. "What do you know of this?"

"Nothing, My Lord. But I fear it is the Doge's assassin whom I mentioned."

The Khan nodded. "I have sent a patrol out to capture him. I believe a slow shredding on the Wooden Donkey would cure him of his obsession."

Later, Marco sat on a hill in the Khan's garden from where he could see the Bell Tower in one direction, the Drum Tower in the other.

Across the field, Marco noticed Rashid approaching. They waved to each other and the Arab trotted up the hill.

"The Khan wants us in his chambers."

"More peasants bearing rumours?"

Rashid eyed Marco. "The assassin is not a rumour. Do not make that mistake."

I meet the Khan's Muslim adviser, Mahmood. The Khan heaps praises on him and says there is no better functionary in his land, no one who could be so skilled at keeping the coffers filled with silver and gold. Mahmood bows his high, thin head deeply, and says he is a humble man, a willing servant, that is all. Yet, there is something unsettling in his manner, and I begin to suspect, but as yet have no proof.

Under a slit-eyed moon, Marco follows the messenger to the Khan's chambers. As usual on entering he is handed white slippers and a small spittoon.

"Sit at my feet, Marco Polo."

Marco does as instructed, and sees that the only other person in the room, seated next to the Khan, is Mahmood.

"I have seen your skill– now I want you to listen. Listen closely to my court. Tell me what they whisper in far corners, between sips of tea, tell me what they say under their blankets, tell me what they say to themselves in their sleep. Listen, and tell me if any are weaving plots against me. Listen to my sons, my daughters, even my wives, my concubines, my eunuchs– especially my eunuchs."

Marco bows his head and closes his eyes. Crickets can be heard in the gardens, and occasionally a few nightbirds chirping or seeming to weep in throaty gasps. After a while, Marco raises his head. "I hear nothing suspicious, My Lord. Merely normal conversations."

"No. No, no. Listen again. One in his dreams turns against me. I know it."

The Khan turns to Mahmood and they whisper together for a few moments. "That is enough for tonight. But I will call on you in the future to assist me again."

The Khan sends me to the south, to Nan-ghin, to check on his realms. The sight of blood has never disturbed me, but the sound of that monkey's screams in Nan-ghin cuts through me still.

The hands of Chien-Ho, the governor, disappeared inside the wide sleeves of his robe. He paced back and forth in the airy sunlit room. Marco could see the sky through the window, strokes and swirls of mare's tail clouds high up under the blue dome of early summer.

"Does he not understand how demeaning it is to the Chinese that he send his officials here? We pay our tribute. What more could he ask? But I shall bite my tongue and say no more about this distasteful subject. No one here is starving, as you can see, but the people in the countryside are poor enough, and our merchants rail against the taxes on their silk. But the tribute must be paid. I tell them it is worth it to keep the Tartars from our doors. Thus far they have listened to me, but if more and more and yet more is asked of the people, they will begin to doubt me and the Khan will get no tribute at all. And then, I can see our river deep with blood. This, I wish to avoid." He was silent.

Chien-Ho turned, raised a finger as he looked at Marco. "You are a Christian, you say, from the West? I know little of your people, but since you are my guests, you must tell me of these distant places. We shall have tea now, and talk later about what message you can take back to the Khan."

Later, as they were bowing to their bowls of tea, Chien-Ho said, "Please do not misunderstand me. I believe the Khan is a wise ruler, but he must know the position I am in here, caught between the fulling-block and the mallet. I have little room to move. We Chinese have few choices left. Many of the intellectuals have become hermits in the mountains rather than live under Tartar rule. A few have gone to the capital to try to work with the Tartars. There is some bad feeling about this. My friend, the great painter, Chao Meng-Fu, went to the capital and now paints in the Khan's court. Did you see him there, painting pictures of horses for the Khan?"

Rashid nodded. "Yes, we met him."

"His horses, though only of pigment or ink, are alive. You can hear them breathing, see their muscles ripple, the nostrils moisten."

Rashid nodded again. "This is true."

Marco concurred.

"Many here despise Chao Meng-Fu for his actions. They say he is a traitor. I have defended him, but not too vociferously. It would be dangerous. There are some here who harbour a powerful hatred for those who have gone north. But I say, each to his own, we must live." He smiled and his hands curled into his wide sleeves.

As Marco and Rashid took their leave, Chien-Ho stepped out into the moist night. "Lest I forget, tomorrow is the Dragon-Boat Festival, a great and ancient event in our city. You will attend as my guests."

The next morning, Marco and Rashid woke to a fine steady rain, what Chien-Ho would later call a "plum rain," good for the crops. A heavy mist filled the air, so thick that Marco could see no more than several feet through his window.

Rashid stood next to him and looked out. "Perhaps it will clear when the sun is higher," but, as if in response, the rain fell harder and the clouds settled lower and mist seemed to rise thicker from the earth itself.

As they walked through the foggy town, two attendants held bamboo umbrellas over the heads of Chien-Ho and the guests. Chien-Ho had brought along his pet monkey on a leash. The animal darted along nervously by his side, its long curled hands in constant motion about its mouth and head. Disembodied voices passed to and fro, the sounds amplified in a peculiar echoey way, as Chien-Ho told his guests about the festival. "Long ago, there lived in this city a well-loved and respected young Mandarin named Wat-yune. On this day in early summer, he drowned in the wide place in our river and many boats went out to look for him. The people lamented, the women wept, the hearts of the men were heavy, for it seemed a bad portent. It was important to find the body of Wat-yune and send it off to the world of the immortals with the honours it deserved. But we never found the young Mandarin. We look for him still, every year on this day. The people go out in boats painted with dragons and search the river in the hopes that some day Wat-yune will be found and his soul will be appeased."

Chien-Ho stopped and looked about. "It is so foggy I have lost my way, though I know the direction well." He looked behind, the way they had come. Nearby a man stood on a doorstep picking his teeth and watching the passersby. Chien-Ho asked the direction and the man pointed, then went back to picking his teeth. They soon came to a gate. "Ah, here we are."

They passed through into the countryside, which was, if anything, mistier still. The air grew thick and grey as they approached the shore of the lake where they could hear a bustle of activity and discern ghostly shapes moving about under a forest of umbrellas, readying boats, pushing off into the water with clunking, slippery sounds. High above, lazy red banners a hundred feet long stitched in and out of the fog.

In a sinuous red and gold boat, they slid onto the water which appeared smooth as oil. The rain increased, pinging onto the bamboo umbrellas and the boat's hull, skithering across the water's surface the colour of pearl and lead, a dusky opalescent skin. Marco could not see to the far end of the boat where Chien-Ho sat. A few feet away he could barely discern the dark profile of Rashid. Between him and Rashid sat the servant trying to protect both of them with the umbrella in his hand but, in his indecision, protecting neither.

All around him Marco could hear the beating of drums and the clangour of discordant music, voices shouting and singing. He leaned over and looked into the water to see if he could see the face of Wat-yune. He was startled by his own face staring back, not from the surface, but from the depths. It seemed to be sinking away from him.

Even with the carnival of sounds around him, Marco

heard nearby the distinct metallic *shring* of someone unsheathing a sword and saw a glint deep in the water. Without thinking he leapt across the lap of the attendant as the sword came down, shattering the gunwale where he had just been sitting. A shout went up. The monkey screamed. The sword came down again as the boats bumped together and the attendant's arm, still holding the umbrella in its hand, went flying off into the water, where it floated away like an aquatic mushroom. Rashid had his sword out and was flailing at the misty air, uselessly, as the attacker's boat had disappeared into the mist. The servant lay screaming and bleeding in the bottom of the boat and was attended to by the other servant who jammed his shirt into the bloody stump. Meanwhile, the monkey kept screaming and running back and forth at its end of the boat.

Chien-Ho, after ensuring that his guests were unhurt, took to the oars himself. "We must return immediately. They know you are the representatives of the Khan. That is why they attacked you. I am most sorry about this. We must return."

Marco wondered if Chien-Ho was correct. Was the assailant indeed an enemy of the Khan? Or was it his own personal enemy, his private shadow stalking him still?

No more attacks came that day, nor during the next six weeks that Marco and Rashid spent with Chien-Ho, surveying the area and learning what they could about the place. It was with heavy hearts they took their leave of Chien-Ho, of whom they had grown fond.

On their return to the capital they reported to the Khan, who congratulated them on their work. "I will neither raise nor lower their tribute. Your work, both of you, has been excellent. Your reports are thorough and you have lived to tell the tale, so luck must also be on your side."

Marco and Rashid bowed.

"With the coming of next spring, Marco Polo, you will take up your duties as the Master of Salt, as I said, in the great city of Hang-chow. In the meantime, make yourselves comfortable as my guests, join me in my feasts and hunts throughout this autumn and winter. The spring will bring another life for you."

In this city where I have been sent to be the Master of Salt, I hear that the Khan's men have been unable to apprehend the assassin. He escapes again and again, as if he is made of mist that dissolves between mountains, as if he is a character in a story that takes unexpected turns.

And now this. Rashid's own personal assassin has found him. The fever is always worst at night. The fever deepens, the victim moans and calls for water, curses the desert from his sleep. Each night, night after night, the same dying deeper and deeper into darkness. I go temporarily mad with grief.

Marco sat in a low chair staring at Rashid as he lay ill in the bed, his lips and tips of fingers black. No one knew what disease had struck the Arab down with such astonishing ferocity.

Rashid moaned and opened his blank eyes. Marco leaned forward with a porcelain cup of water. By the time the cup touched the Arab's lips, he had slipped away again, back into his dying, wasting sleep. Not a sleep that refreshes, but the kind that slowly sucks out life.

With a cloth, Marco wiped the sweat from his own brow, licked his lips and tasted salt. He wiped Rashid's face, sweat gathering in the welter of wrinkles. The Arab's mouth hung open, his tongue black as a well. The Chinese doctors had said they could do nothing. They said the end would come quickly. But, they underestimated the strength of this one from the desert. Marco drank from his own cup. The air was still in the closed-up room. He stood and walked to the window. As he pulled back the green gauze at the window, he heard the final gurgling in Rashid's throat. He felt his heart freeze and his own breath catch as he turned. Behind him, from deep in the forest of bamboo, a warbler trilled a rising phrase against the silence. Marco looked again outside.

Dawn was caught low in the branches. He thought he saw a shadow weaving through the grove. In the half-light he snatched up his sword and leapt out the door. In a sudden rage, he slashed at shadows slanting among the bamboo stalks tumbling in piles. He spun around. His face sweaty and contorted, he slashed again, and again, and again.

A servant-boy, half-dressed, came running out from the house. "Master, master! What is it? Are you mad?"

Marco shouted and hacked to the left, then the right, toppling bamboo canes in heaps, he could not stop, his hands moving of their own accord, his arms swinging the sword high over his head.

"I must root these shadows out if I have to cut down the entire forest!"

The servant-boy ran back into the house to wake an older servant, but by the time they returned Marco lay on his back among the bamboo canes, his eyes wide open, crumbling moans forcing themselves out of his chest, his face soaked with tears.

A Jail Cell In Genoa (IV)

Rusticello continues to bait me, speaks incessantly of this and that, weaves such labyrinths of words that I am as lost in my narrow cell as ever I was in high mountain valley or trackless desert.

Marco and Rusticello finished eating their bread, a bit of greens in olive oil, a small chunk of greasy salt pork. "God in Heaven, what I wouldn't give for a brazier to ward off this damp." Rusticello paced about, hugging himself. Marco ignored him.

The rest of the day the Pisan spent softly singing Provencal songs: a long nonsensical *flabel*, a satirical *estribot* a plaintive and sad *planh*. He closed at dusk with a *serena* so tender and gentle it brought a tear to his eye. The Venetian seemed to enjoy the songs but said not a word, merely stared out the square window at afternoon's shimmering glow, at pale yellow twilight, at gathering night.

Marco spat out the words in anger. "Your damned enthusiasms are utterly deluded. You think everything in this world should be of interest. Well, I've seen the world and it's a low and ugly place, filled with people stuffing their gullets and gouging each others' eyes out. You think every blade of grass, every passing cloud, every bird feather, is worth investigating. None of these mean anything– life is empty of meaning. All that keeps me going is the slimmest thread of curiosity about how empty it can get. You astound me with your false gentleness, your fake kindness to the fleas that infest your bed. Given half a chance, they would eat you down to the bone."

Rusticello held up his hand, palm out.

Marco fell into a sullen silence, gazing at the door to their cell.

"For you, the door is the saving grace, you stare at it and your heart fills with hope and fear. You seem to cling to that struggle. You have stopped staring at the window and now stare only at the door. Have you noticed? For me, the saving grace remains the window, a small simple miracle, at this moment filled with blue."

Marco continued staring at the door, as if addressing his words to its steadfast blankness. "What I do not understand is why my family has not yet bought my freedom? I am a wealthy man. What keeps them? What holds them back?"

"Perhaps you never went beyond the Levant and made the entire story up using a Persian source." Rusticello was talking again. Marco barely listened. "Anything is possible, is it not? As much has been done by others. What about the tales of Federico Galdiano concerning the paradise across the western sea? Or the fantastic tales of Murshid Asadu 'llah who claimed to have visited a city deep under the earth?"

"So what if I have made it up?"

Rusticello looked puzzled and for once was struck dumb, not so much by the question, but by the colour of the Venetian's tongue. He pointed. "Your tongue, it's black. Why? Are you ill? I have seen black tongues before, but only on those near death. You, however, look as healthy today as you did yesterday. A bit thin, perhaps, from our meagre fare, but healthy for a man of forty-five years."

"Your tongue also is black, you blathering knave. I hope it soon falls out so that I might have a moment's peace."

Rusticello, startled, put his hand to his mouth. Marco shook his head. "Don't fret, fool, it's simply from the squid-ink soup we ate last night. That soup made me think of home. I dreamt of Venice last night, dreamt of my old father, smelled the sea, saw the light reflecting up from the canal and shimmering on the ceiling of a room in our house. At a time like this," he said, gazing around the cell, "I wish I had no memory at all." Marco sat down in silence while Rusticello gazed out the window.

The Venetian's shoulders sank further and further, the sockets of his eyes filled with shadow, as if the blackness of his tongue were spreading and filling up his head, the room, the very air. Rusticello awaited the inevitable explosion. In late afternoon, it came.

Marco leaps to his feet without warning, runs to the door and starts pounding with both fists. "Forty-five years! I have accomplished nothing, done nothing, am nothing!" He pounds his fists, working himself into a rage, spins and runs full speed for the stone wall opposite the door, flinging himself against it, smashing his face and bloodying his lip, knocking himself to the floor. He leaps up, runs across the room, throws himself again hard against the door. A bit of something strikes Rusticello in the forehead as he watches in stunned dismay. Reaching out, he picks up a broken tooth from the floor. Marco runs for the back wall again. "Stop! In the name of God, stop!" Rusticello stands and rushes to block Marco's path. The two collide and fall to the floor where Rusticello lies on top of the Venetian, his extra forty pounds helping subdue Marco, who lies still, blood coming from his nose and mouth, tears oozing from the corners of his eyes. "Stop," Rusticello whispers. "Stop."

In late afternoon, a slow rain began to fall. It was mid-autumn.

"Don't you see, my friend? The invention of purgatory is

the beginning of the end for Mother Church, for purgatory is where we live, now, on this earth. Why do we need another world, a kind of anteroom to heaven? As the Lord is my witness, Christ Jesus never spoke of any purgatory. Did he?"

"Rusticello, you come up with one strange and dangerous heresy after another. It is a form of entertainment with you."

Rusticello ignored him. "And further, I have studied several maps that show the Earthly Paradise to be out beyond the distant East. Is it true? Is it there?"

"There is no innocence so foolish as that of the scholar." Marco, pacing in the cramped cell, smiled down at Rusticello.

"And no cynicism so sad as that of the practical man," the Pisan shot back.

Marco stopped and glanced at the high shelf over Rusticello's pile of straw. "Your ink— it has gone dry in its bottle, cracked like a riverbed in the hot season."

"Yes, I know. A simple alchemy should change that. A bit of moisture, the Lord be served, will bring it to life— have no fear."

Marco continued pacing, gazing at the floor. "So, you believe we already dwell in purgatory?"

"It is something we had to invent. Your grandfather's grandfather never heard of purgatory. Consider the six directions: east, west, north, south, heaven and hell. There remains no place for purgatory to be but here." Rusticello pointed at his own chest.

"Why?" Marco stopped again and looked at Rusticello. "Why now?"

"I don't know."

"Why now, when men are learning that the world is not what they thought? When travellers return from distant lands where none have gone before, when the old world is shattered, a time when maps are more useless and transitory than clouds? A time when many cry out that apocalypse closes on us like a low dark cloud. Why did we come to need a purgatory now?"

"It came from the city of Paris–the invention of a feverish half-mad spiritual mind. The work likely of the notorious forger, Nicholas of Clairvaux, the Holy Bernard's secretary. Perhaps he felt caught between heaven and hell, stuck here as we all are, truly, between beast and angel."

"Caught between the great journey..." Marco mumbled, even as Rusticello looked up and said, "...and the locked cell."

Figure Eight

Back in the Khan's winter capital, I ponder the emptiness of the world. How will I continue to protect myself without the help of Rashid, poor Rashid, my friend, my companion? Meanwhile, I am visited by a dwarf eunuch from the Khan's harem.

Snow started to fall, slowly at first, then thickening until half the air filled with white puffs. Staring from his chamber in the Khan's palace, Marco watched snow collect in the willows and maples in the imperial gardens, filling up the curling pathways and dissolving in the lake. Since returning from Hang-chow Marco had spent many hours staring out into the blue air, grey air, black. Sometimes all day, sometimes half the night.

Nothing for me here. Nothing.

A half-dozen plump birds, soft dark grey, pumped past his vision. He watched as flakes of snow drifted into the black lake.

"Man from the West."

Marco turned from the view to see an odd little creature standing in his room by the door. He was about three feet tall and three feet wide and was dressed like a juggler from the Khan's court.

"Who are you?"

"I have a name. But it is not my name."

"A riddler then?"

"Yes, a riddler, and much more besides."

"And what would that be?"

"As you can see by my dress I am a juggler and acrobat of the Khan's harem."

"A eunuch then?"

"Supposedly. I am also an ambassador of magic and gramarye, an alchemist, a mechanic skilled in the use of machines of entertainment as well as devices of illusion. I am also a leech and a star-clerk, but few know of this. Everyone watches me perform for them, but none know me. I have knowledge of ivory, rhinoceros horn and tortoise-shell, none of which will help you, nor the Khan, out of your current dilemmas. Unlike the elder Polos I know nothing of jewels. I *do* conjure, spit fire, dance with a thousand and one balls and interchange the heads of cows and horses."

The little eunuch was never still, rocking from foot to foot, the small curved knife at his belt in its jeweled scabbard swinging. Suddenly he tucked his chin into his chest, leaned forward and rolled like a ball, somersaulting again onto his feet.

"You strike me as having the looks of a Hindu. Are you from those lands?"

"Yes. There is also the blood of Mongols and Chinese in my veins. My mother a Hindu, my father a Muslim. Beyond that, no one knows."

"What is it you want?"

"Your thoughts."

Marco tilted his head and stared. "What?"

"I feast on thoughts. I eat them, good or bad. But the thoughts of a man or woman in deep sorrow are particularly rich and delicious. I want to eat your sad thoughts. That is why I can never be still. Because I am so filled with the energy of thoughts, I tumble and run like a rodent. I juggle with the heads of a thousand and one birds swallowing their thoughts of flight even as they rise and fall through the air."

"And how do you propose to eat my thoughts?"

"You will see in a moment. But first, did you not wish to

138

ask me something about the harem?"

Marco shook his head, as if startled. "Yes, yes I did. You said before, in answering my question about whether you are a eunuch, you said, 'supposedly'. What mean you by that?"

"I am indeed a guard of the Imperial couch, but when they first came to cut me, having control over such things I hid my manhood inside my body. They said I was naturally born to the harem. Despite my size, my jeweled stem is the equal of any emperor's." His black eyes twinkled. "Each night I make my rounds under cover of dark, imitating the Khan's voice, having my choice of the harem's delicacies. In the morning I tumble for them, and juggle, and swallow their sweet thoughts."

"And my thoughts— have you eaten them too?"

"Oh, yes, every last one, the heavy sad ones, and the sweet-tasting light ones. For me your thoughts have the taste of the exotic, being from so far off, from such a distant land. And a bit salty too, I must add, from your time spent at sea, no doubt."

Marco nodded. "Are you a ghost?"

The little man laughed. "No. Nor demon. Neither am I incubus, and certainly not succubus. I am not made of spirit but flesh, blood and bone like any man. All of us under the sign of Death branded invisibly on our foreheads. But I must return." Walking to the door, he paused. "One more thing. You can call me Adim."

One green and shining day, I visit the Imperial Silkworm Gardens with Adim. In the mottled light, I learn that all opposites have a point of connection, as in a figure-eight: day and

night, waking and dreams, myself and the assassin.

Marco stood with Adim outside the walls of the Imperial Silkworm Gardens. He watched as an old man, grasping a long arced wooden pole, lowered a clay pot into a well. To the astonishment of Marco and Adim, he raised the pot brimming with clear sparkling water which he dumped into a basket at his feet. "A basket!" Marco turned to Adim. "Is he mad? The water runs into the ground." Adim, a puzzled look on his face, shrugged his shoulders.

Adim and Marco stepped past a guard and through a door in the high stone wall– Marco looking both ways along the outside of the wall could see neither its beginning nor its end– and entered the Imperial Silkworm Garden. Once inside, Marco saw that the walls around the garden formed a huge square within which a forest of mulberry trees grew. At the end of the well-worn path heading to the garden's center he saw a compact wooden building which he surmised was a silkworm breeding house.

Adim, his bamboo staff marking the dirt of the path, held to his silence as they walked.

Other than the workers, only those most intimately involved with the affairs of state were allowed access to the gardens, for silk was valued as highly as silver or gold. Those who worked the imperial gardens lived apart from the world so they could never divulge the secrets of the royal cocoons.

Adim halted. "Look...here." He ran his hand along the bark of a tree. "We have joined two kinds of mulberry in one."

It was the peak of spring, the rounded heart-shapes of the serrated mulberry leaves a dark rich green sparkling in the sunshine and flickering in the sensuous breeze speckled with birdsong.

"We have taken the wild mulberry with its strong trunk and root and joined it to the farmer's mulberry with its larger leaves. We want a smaller tree so the harvesting girls can pick more easily. And yet we want a tree that has more leaf to feed to the silkworms. You see– we have taken the wild and joined it to the cultivated, and so we improve things."

They arrived at the small clearing before the breeding house and sat on a stone bench. Here the mulberry trees were huge and ancient, the mottled sunlight flickered on the ground. Marco felt as if he were inside a cathedral or great temple, the air hushed and clear and radiant.

Adim leaned forward and drew a square in the dirt with the tip of his bamboo staff. Inside the square he drew two bisecting lines, dividing the square into four perfect inner squares. "*Thien*," he said. "The Chinese character for field, the shape of the girls' baskets, the shape of the garden. Four quadrants. Within this order, chaos is charmed and learns to serve."

"Tell me, Adim. You have spoken of the way of the silkworm. What is it?"

"Egg, caterpillar, chrysalis, moth. We say it begins with the egg but the egg came from the moth and the moth from the chrysalis and so on. The cycle is eternal, with no beginning and no end. The silkworm moves its head about continuously in a figure-eight pattern in constructing its cocoon, ejecting a thin filament of silk from its mouth."

"Silk flows from their mouths, you say? So, it is the tale they have to tell."

"Yes. Only a few breeding moths are allowed to hatch from the cocoon, however, for hatching severs the threads and ruins the silk. Those allowed to hatch lay their eggs on a mulberry leaf and the cycle begins anew."

"The chrysalis must be killed inside the cocoon? How?"

"With heat, applied at the correct time. The way of the silkworm depends on time. Without time's order there would simply be worms and eggs and moths. No silk."

They sat in silence and watched as three girls approached along the path, each with jet black hair hanging down her back where it was tied with a double-looped bow. One carried a hooked stick for pulling down the mulberry branches. They smiled shyly and disappeared into the house with their full baskets of leaves.

"What is inside the house?" asks Marco.

"Silkworm mats, trays, a heating stove, all the necessary apparatus for the breeding of silkworms, and...."

The eunuch stops. Leaning on his staff he gazes into the distant blue sky studded with high white clouds.

"And that is all, nothing else?"

Adim turns and looks at Marco, his sad grey eyes measuring this young man from the other side of the world. "At the center of the square house there is an altar that holds a book with red silk covers. Very old. It would certainly crumble into dust if you were to touch it."

"And what is in the book?"

"A riddle. The riddle of the figure-eight– the world on one side..." Adim pauses and thinks.

"And, on the other side?"

"Another world, dreams, stories, the imagination...it depends. You– and the one who seeks to destroy you."

"We are connected then, the assassin and I. What connects us?"

"That itself is the riddle."

"Might I see this book?" Marco is already rising to enter the house.

"No. It is not allowed. No one may see the book. Not

even Confucius. Not even the Buddha."

"Then," Marco settles back down onto the bench, "how is it you know what is in the book?"

"I don't. I imagine it. It is all the same to me."

The girls exited the house, their baskets now empty, and passed again. "I will tell you the story of the Empress and the Lion," Adim said when the girls had gone. "It was long ago. I will leave it to you to decide if the story is myth or one of those tales about the world that reveals a hidden truth."

"Once, near the beginning of time, an Empress was about to give birth. She demanded that she be brought to this very garden. On passing through the stone wall, her ladies-in-waiting saw that the birth pains had begun and a messenger was sent for the midwives. Under a towering mulberry tree, she fell asleep three times and awoke three times. During each sleep many strange and magical events occurred. The sky darkened, as in an eclipse of the sun. A flock of ducks was seen to fly backwards. A stream that flows through the garden ceased flowing and turned the muted opalescent colour of raw silk. Leaves on the mulberry tree above her turned into swallows and flew away. A water-clock in the breeding house for no reason stopped dripping.

"A sage present at the birth told the frightened women that time had been stilled, that outer time had become disengaged, while inner time continued moving toward its fruition. The women did not understand, and were frightened even further when the Empress gave birth to what appeared to be a child wrapped in a silk cocoon. But they could see, under the taut white sac, that it wasn't a child but a beast of some sort breaking through the translucent skin. It grew larger and larger and, when the sac tore, they stood staring at what lay still on the ground before them. A dragon– half-eagle, half-lion– w rought of gold.

"When the Emperor heard of the miraculous birth, he had the winged beast placed on the altar at the center of the silkworm breeding house. But inner time and outer were disengaged during the birth, as the sage had said, with the result that the silkworm oracle's prediction for the hatching of the moths was incorrect. The breeding house was filled with silkworm cocoons that should have been killed with heat at the appropriate time. Instead, the delay allowed the hatching of hundreds of thousands of moths in the house. The collective thrum of their wings lifted the house with the golden dragon into the heavens where it disappeared in the clouds. The house you see now was built at a later time."

After a moment's silence, Adim leapt up from his seat and headed along the path. Marco joined him and, as the sun began to fade and dissolve behind the tangle of branches, they walked under the overarching mulberry trees.

Outside the walls, Marco noted that the old man still had not succeeded in filling his basket with water.

Once again, I sense that I am caught in a story that turns in upon itself. Nothing is as it seems– east is west and west is east, and there is but one channel that leads from one to the other. If the assassin passes through those narrows first, all is lost. If I, by the grace of God and the Virgin, pass through first, I will have defeated him.

Adim paced back and forth in Marco's chambers, shaking his head. "He is here. He has penetrated to the very heart of the court, and whispers against you in willing ears."

"Yes– I have not seen him, but I know he has arrived. I hear him, the whispering goes on all night, like a black icicle, dripping."

"Indeed, he has a great talent for evil, this one."

"Whose ear does he have?"

"The Muslim, Mahmood's."

"I thought you said his power would soon wane."

"I did, I admit it." Adim continued to pace. "Fate has been delayed by the arrival of your assassin."

"How is it no one knows he is here?"

"He has a certain magic, a miraculous power. He appears as he wishes."

"No. He has no magic. There is no truth in this."

"Don't deny it. Do not underestimate him. That would be a grave error."

Marco went to the window and stared out at the dusk. "Damn it!" He pounded with his right fist on the wall beside the window. "The devil take him!"

With a quick somersault, Adim was standing next to Marco. He put his hand over his mouth and spoke softly. "Never stop listening for him. It is your only defense. As for Mahmood the Intriguer, his fate is sealed. Your fate, on the other hand, is too intertwined with your evil countryman's for me to discern. Once again, the Khan's plans for you will intervene. You will go with him to a battle in the north. You will be safer there under a rain of arrows than in this court while the Khan is gone."

As we head for the battleground in the north, the Khan tells me I look grey and worried, thinking I fear the coming battle.

I cannot tell him I fear more what comes from behind than what waits ahead. I have seen many battles and begin to tire of this sport. Here is the forest of tragedy, weeping pines, torn poplars, beasts gone mad.

From a distance of thirty *li*, Marco could see the pillars of smoke holding up the grey sky. Pulling up on the reins and leaning toward the Khan, he pointed. The Khan's constant frown deepened in his jowled face. "Funeral pyres beyond the field of battle– the enemy is burning his dead."

Marco nodded slowly. The constant pounding of hooves and the passage of tens of thousands of infantry had beaten the earth into a dry wasteland. To their left stood a forest of pine, grey with dust. Out of the distance ahead came riding a contingent of Mongol soldiers, each with a pair of red silk streamers trailing from his helmet.

The main column, a thousand horsemen strong, halted as the general and two guards broke off from the smaller group and rode up to the Khan. Dismounting with ease, they stood, heads bowed, at the Khan's feet. "General Li, how goes the battle?"

"A thousand blessings on you, My Lord. The two armies are ranged along the opposite sides of the next valley. We only await your order to attack. Your camp is nearby and all is prepared. I have no doubt, Your Majesty, that we will vanquish them, for our numbers are greater, our skill superior, our leaders by far the bravest."

"Yes, yes. Ride ahead and secure us a vantage point above the valley."

"It is already accomplished, Your Majesty."

General Li and his two lieutenants leapt onto their horses and rode off. The Khan, reining in his restless horse, watched the horsemen disappear in the distance. Around him the column shifted, awaiting his word to move on. "I fear my general is a fool." He looked at Marco seriously. "A skilled fool, even a brave fool, but a fool nonetheless. What think you, Marco? To the attack? Or is another disaster awaiting us?"

"My Lord, I know little of the situation. What do your advisors say?"

"My advisors? I can no longer hear them. They make my ears ring and my feet hurt. My most trusted concubine, Chiga, wants me to bring her the head of our esteemed enemy, Prince Nayan the traitor. She understands nothing of the situation, of course. If we lose this valley, Nayan's forces will enter a region where many of the peasants support him. They will be able to move quickly then, and I fear will threaten my capital by the fall. We must halt them here, now. Let us ride."

With a slight nod from the Khan to his flagman, the column of the imperial horseguard began moving. "I am too old for another battle. I have seventy-two years, Marco. My sword grows heavy in my hand. I look around and wonder who will be dead by tomorrow's eve."

The Khan lapsed into silence. Marco glanced out of the corner of his eye at him. His wide jowly face was covered in red blotches. His enormous form weighed down his horse.

As they sat on their horses above the valley Marco thought the Khan looked all-powerful in his armour which shone with the brilliance of the sun. But the thought struck him that it was a late-afternoon sun, low on the horizon. He knew the soldiers would look from the valley to the Khan on his great horse halfway up the hillside behind them and they would marvel at the radiance of their emperor. But the dragon swirling about his filigreed gold helmet was a spent force, spinning in circles, going nowhere.

The Khan raised his right hand in the air, then stopped and lowered it slowly. A lone horse had run out onto the field between the opposing armies. A handsome horse, deep rich grey with an oiled black tail and slick black mane. It was impossible to tell which side the horse had come from. But it was easy enough to see that the beast had gone mad. It ran back and forth in a fury, throwing its head from side to side as if trying to remove something from its back, a bloody foam coming from the mouth, its eyes enormous.

The Khan, on his own horse with its gold and purple silk trappings, surrounded by his imperial troops, said, "The beast feels the fear. It senses the future of this place, when the soil of the valley will be soaked a sword's depth with blood."

"Look." Marco pointed.

From the end of the valley, a single warrior walked out from behind the loose stone piles and began warily to approach the beast. "It is Nayan himself." The Khan told the flagman to signal the troops to hold their arrows.

With a round silver shield on his arm, the prince moved with the grace of a young lion. As Nayan walked slowly across the field, Marco could sense his pride, his contained disciplined power. The horse raged back and forth, rearing up to kick its front legs at the air, its eyes bulging. As Nayan approached with caution, he turned his shield aside so a sudden flash would not frighten the beast. Nayan carried no weapon but stroked the air with his empty right hand.

"The prince is calling to him." The Khan's eyes were riveted on the figure in the field. The valley was silent but for the calling of crows high on the hills.

The horse had stopped running. A long string of foamy spittle hung from its mouth down to the ground. Its ears perked. As Nayan drew close, the beast stepped back. Nayan with his hand raised in front of him kept caressing the air in a placating motion. He stepped closer again. The horse shied, again perked its ears. Nayan placed his hand on the beast's neck and stroked it. The horse relaxed and Nayan turned and began to lead the horse off the field. At that moment it happened.

Even the crows ceased their complaints. An uncanny silence penetrated every stone, every dry blade of grass, every soldier's thoughts. A moment of silence so deep it filled the air with unimaginable energy and power, as if the empty light itself had somehow come alive and brightened, as if Nayan's silver shield were reflecting the glare of the sun into every man's eyes.

An arrow arced out of nowhere– it could have come from either side of the valley– missed the prince by inches and lodged deep in the horse's right eye. The beast let out a great cry, kicked out at Nayan, missing him, and began swinging its lowered head side to side as it stumbled about the field.

The Khan rose up in his saddle and looked about to see if he could locate the source of the arrow, but it was impossible. He sat down, gritted his teeth and nodded to the flagman on his left. When the flagman waved a red banner in the air, the sky was instantly filled with arrows and the silence was shattered with terrible cries.

I tire of this palace, this fetid overwrought court. I spend each evening sitting at the feet of the Khan, my head bowed, listening to the fervour of intrigue. Mahmood has confirmed my worst

suspicions. I must leave, even if it puts me at the mercy of the assassin. I must quit this city. I must.

"Who passes?" The voice of the guard came sharply out of the darkness at the wide palace gate.

Adim cocked his head at the sound of the voice but said nothing.

"The younger Polo and the harem eunuch, Adim. The Khan has requested our presence," Marco said.

It seemed odd to Marco that the guard was standing out of the moonlight, half-way behind the high bamboo gate.

Suddenly Marco felt Adim jerk on his arm with such force that he went flying and tumbled to the ground. In the same moment, moonlight flickered along a blade as it flashed and sparked off the cobbles where Marco had just stood. By the time Marco and Adim had their own blades out, the sound of the assailant's retreat was a distant echo.

Inside the gate they found the bodies of the two regular guards. Blood glistened from their bamboo chest armour and still oozed from their expertly slit throats.

Marco wandered a short distance away and collapsed against a wall. Adim paced back and forth in front of him. "This is not the work of Mahmood and his web of spies— and yet the chaos he has brought to the court makes it possible. You must leave for good. Return to your home. The Khan cannot control things much longer. He is failing. Once he is gone, your enemies will crawl from their hiding places and find you in the full light of day. Return. Return now."

In the middle of the night I wake in a sweat, my breath coming

in jagged bursts, the dream flooding back in with chaotic light.

I have seen him. I have spoken to the assassin. "What has my father done? What have I done that makes me worthy of your tireless searching? We are innocent. Why do you hound us?"

The assassin spoke and in his speech it grew clear to me that he was as driven by fate as any stream in its bed or machine in its works. "My orders are beyond guilt and innocence. I am like a water clock; I go on dripping, despite the season, without regard to changes in the political winds, without reference to anyone's wishes or wants– whether those of king or common man. As for your father, he no longer interests me. One cannot get blood from old leather. It is you I seek."

In the silence of hollow night, I understood him at last– and feared him the more.

Across the wide plain Marco rode with Niccolo and the Khan and his retinue of three dozen guards toward a stand of willow trees. Above and beyond the line of horsemen, ranging along the horizon, ran a frieze of towering clouds. Past the willows, the flat landscape rose into a long low hill.

The party left the capital early in the morning and rode hard, imperial flags flapping. They had covered the first fifty *li* of the journey by noon. The Khan and the Polos rode in silence in the middle of the pack. A line of clouds massed along the horizon beyond them, looking like a great white city of palaces and towers and turrets, crenellated battlements and slowly drifting walls and ramparts; a city disappearing into its own silence, dissolving in the wind.

Under the willow trees they reined in their horses and dismounted. The Khan wore riding robes of yellow silk and a sword with a sharkskin-covered hilt. His face tumescent and purplish, he gave orders for the main party to wait while he and the foreigners went on.

Marco and Niccolo walked on each side of the Khan, while three guards in light chain mail followed close behind. Over the hill, they came upon another plain covered in barley that reached to their knees. At the mound's foot, a lone maple tree stretched its extravagant limbs, not up into the air but out, as if trying to touch the horizon's edge.

The Khan shaded his eyes and pointed.

When the party reached the tree, the emperor instructed the three guards to wait as he walked on with Marco and his father.

They walked several *li* into the field and the Khan stopped. "There." He approached what appeared to be a slab of stone visible just below the heads of barley, the rock mottled with pink, green and pale blue rosettes of lichen. Stepping up onto the slab, he surveyed the fields where wind shivered through the grain. "Beneath this earth are the ruins of a palace. On this spot, kings with armies of servants held sway, feasted, loved their queens and concubines, planned campaigns with their generals, punished traitors. Now, nothing."

The wind whipped through his yellow robes, ran in rivulets through the barley.

"Why?! Why is it– you must tell me again– why is it you wish to leave?"

The Khan stepped down heavily from the stone and began pacing back and forth in front of the other two, his gaze down as he listened.

Marco spoke. "It is time to return, Your Majesty. You have been more than generous, and your kindness knows no bounds, but we must leave." Marco looked at his father.

The Khan continued to pace back and forth, then stopped abruptly. He drew his sword with a clear metallic ring, a shocking sound under the vast and empty sky. Grasping the hilt with both hands, he thrust the sword into the earth, and continued his pacing as the sword swayed slightly on its point.

"You know it cannot be the same when you return. All will have changed, the very earth will have risen or fallen as the gods dictate."

Marco and Niccolo nodded.

"You have served me well," the Khan gazed at Marco. "Indeed, you have been as a son to me. I have offered you double what you now hold in jewels and gold, if you would but stay, and yet you deny me. Four times since the snow season ended I have refused your father's petition to return to the land of his birth because I could not imagine being without your assistance, or your comradeship. But, I begin to understand. You believe I will die soon– no, do not deny it, it is perhaps true– and you think that once I have died your protection here will be gone and you will be at the mercy of whomever follows in my footsteps. Is it not true?"

"Yes, it is partly true."

"Partly true?"

Marco nodded. "More than that. We believe that our return could never be accomplished without your assistance. We would need the mercy of your passage to move through your realms."

Marco watched the Khan continuing to pace, gazing at the ground, his hands opening and closing beneath his wide yellow sleeves. Finally, his nostrils flared as he took in a deep breath and smelled the wind. He approached the sword, gripped it again with two hands and drew it from the earth.

"I have decided. Though I bear in my heart a sorrow as boundless as the sky, I give you leave to go, and in going you will fulfill one more duty on my behalf. Listen well. The emissaries of Argon of India have asked that I allow you to help them return to their land. As you know, I have given Argon what he requested of me– a lovely young maiden of seventeen from among the relatives of my dead queen. The emissaries left with the princess Kogatin eight months ago. Unfortunately, they have recently returned, their progress obstructed by wars along their way. With your help, they wish to attempt the journey again, this time by sea. I have told the three barons that they may have your services as navigators for the journey so long as they assist you in your attempts to return to Venice. And once you have seen your home, you will return to me again, and we will feast and talk through the night and conquer whatever remains of the world to be conquered." The Khan smiled and returned his sword to its scabbard.

"The party will be equipped with fourteen sailing ships, and as many sailors and fighting men as you need. You shall have stores and provisions for two years. And I will furnish you with two golden tablets with instructions that you be provided safe passage through all my dominions. In you I vest the authority to act as my ambassadors to the Pope, the kings of France and Spain, and all the Christian Princes. Now, let us return and feast and drink in sad farewell; let us talk our last talks until dawn or the end of time."

I prepare myself for the journey to come. I know now be will find me. I begin to long to see his face.

Marco sits on the roof of a house under the whirling stars. The Great Dipper tips out a river of darkness sparkling with milk, stars caught in the whirlpool and dizzying around the skirt of the heavens. On the flat roof of the house, Marco, insomniac, leans back, astonished as much at the spacing and pattern of the stars as at their number and brilliance.

In two hours the deep blue of the dawn bell will boom from the base of the Bell Tower. The great machine of time, of which I am an inconsequential piece, will shift a degree, the chronosphere will twist and click, the gears of the sun will catch the gears of the earth and another day will begin, my final one in Cathay. There is no stopping it.

On the black lacquered table before him rest a map and a scroll calendar. The edges of the map– beyond east, west, north and south– are marked Terra Incognita. As he picks up the calendar to consult it by the flickering candlelight, a sudden swirling wind, seeming to come from nowhere and all directions at once, tears the scroll from his hands and spins it into the black amnesiac air, and in the same moment, extinguishes the candle.

Marco, sitting in the sudden dark, hears the distant sound of an arrow rending silk.

With my father and uncle, I inspect the "starry rafts," Chinese junks, rocking in the harbour. The wind is in my hair. I can taste salt. My heart beats and thumps like a sail.

The raked sail of the midship foremast had come loose and wrapped round like a shroud. Marco watched, squinting against the sunlight, as half-a-dozen nimble sailors unwound and adjusted the sail.

"A good wind." Uncle Maffeo smiled at Marco through his blackened teeth, his grey-speckled beard.

The wharf was a bustle of activity and last-minute preparations, men loading provisions for the journey, barrels of rice and fresh water, dried fish and salt. Sailors shouted over the general din of families saying farewell, carts clattering, horses clomping and whinnying. Marco gazed at his father's old lined face. *Now, like me, he looks more Chinese than Venetian.*

"Hello, Man from the West." Marco recognized the voice of Adim, the dwarf tumbler from the Khan's harem. Marco nodded a greeting.

"I have just heard. I too am coming on the journey. I will cook for the princess, and entertain her, and tell stories to the men when the nights are long. But I must hurry. Many provisions yet to load. You will see me again."

He ambled into the crowd and disappeared.

The Polos, the barons and Kogatin with her ladies-in-waiting would travel together on one ship, the largest of the fourteen. The smell of salt wind whipping the sails roused Marco and quickened his blood. He closed his eyes and took a deep breath. On opening them, he saw his father smiling at him.

The Khan had said his farewells, heaped riches on them, many of which they had to leave behind, gifts to trusted servants and friends. Between Niccolo and Maffeo sat a sign of the Khan's munificence: a casket filled with rubies, pearls and other jewels.

Marco and his father often had little to say to each other, but when it came to ships, they had much to discuss. They both inspected the junk with a practiced eye. Marco commented how it appeared slightly unwieldly in the upper works, though the lower and underwater lines of the pinewood hull and its keel–its "dragon bone"–seemed sweet and generally functional. The stem and stern ribs had been grown to their curved shape, cut from special trees for the purpose.

Marco glanced across the waves as his father talked about the ship. Soon they would be on the water. *Once I am at sea,* he thought, *I will already be home.*

A Jail Cell In Genoa (V)

Rusticello has planted himself in my ear like a seed from which grows a fevered vine. Its tendrils are inescapable. I listen hard for a comforting silence but all I hear is his voice stretching inside me.

From his fever, Marco moans and tosses, then falls still and silent. Rusticello, with a cloth, wipes the Venetian's forehead, watches the grey flickering eyelids. Behind the silence, the fever glitters and spills out silent words:

Gold, silver, crystal, agate, lapis lazuli, red pearls, cornelian. The diamond cutter speaks and the silence glitters and a lotus blossoms in his mouth and a black moth flutters out. The house is burning! The house is burning! But the diamond cutter constructed of diamonds, constructed not of words, is untouched. He holds the book scented with incense. Each time he opens it, invisible clouds of incense come drifting out, dry mist of sandalwood, dust of roses. The diamond cutter smiles and worlds are cut in half. White and black. Wet and dry. Dark and light. He holds a torch that lights the cave. Cave multiplying upon cave, cave beyond cave, cave above and below cave, a warren of caves, a honeycomb of caves in the side of a mountain, in the earth. In the fresco on the wall a house is burning. The diamond cutter is showing me a book, his book. It smells like heaven. I think it is the burning house that smells of sandalwood. He speaks and it takes me years to hear his words. They ring like clear chimes in another time, another place. The world is cut in half and upside down, quartered, multiplying. Walls covered in images. Holy men in desert colours. The diamond cutter speaks and maps ripple in circles, in and out of rooms, maps flowing along the walls like water, like stains, leading nowhere, leading inward and down, up and out, tracing figure-eights like knots in a carpet. A hundred *li* south of the Silk Route, in the side of a hill, in Genoa, in fever. These are the maps of my fever. A fever of words, as always. Silk Route in loops of figure-eights. Bound in cocoons of figure-eights. Words that won't speak themselves because they are ashamed. They are only words. The diamond cutter is vomiting up flowers of words that disappear into other caves, echo in distant rooms. The house is burning, burning with fever that smells like sandalwood, that smells like silk dust of roses. He opens the book and the words mist out a thousand years later, it's breathing. The book is breathing but its air isn't air it's words. They're just the words, smelling sweet, holy with perfume. Their silk smoke passes through all the caves in my head, their dust perfumes all the caves in my head, their winds chime all the chimes in my head. I know this is fever, the Pisan with his rough bare hands wipes water on my forehead, but I am stuck in the caves a thousand *li* a hundred *li* south of the Silk Road and the torch burns in the diamond cutter's hand. He told me he was a diamond cutter but the words floated off into the petrified dark of the caves, a cutter of black cabochons he said, so black they shine with a brilliance beyond compare, so brilliant they are burning down the house with a single glance, so brilliant all the flames disappear into them, so black they are smaller than a speck of dust, so brilliant they bring on and cure all fevers, so said the diamond cutter whose mouth opened with blossoms of lotus and whose head was a warren of caves whose walls were covered in paintings of desert-coloured gods and sloe-eyed holy men and maps that showed no way but down and in and out and up, flowing in figure-eights like water through rooms, like stains, like streams of colour in a fever of colour, yellow fever, blue fever, white, black, dust of green, murex jungles at the bottom of the sea of fever, swaying in the wind, dancing like the flames on the tips of his fingers. The house is burning! The house is burning! The lotus in his mouth is on fire. The diamond in the diamond cutter's hand is on fire. I am in the caves a thousand *li* north of the Silk Route, in the side of a hill, in a mountain inside the earth, the caves inside my head. The maps lead me in a fever of circles. I am leaving a trail of silk moths that smell like sandalwood and ripple like fine silk cloth on the river in the sunlight in the dust, a white dust drifting out behind me, a trail of words that hatched from the caves in my head and drifted away back into silence, in distant rooms, though they began in silence, continued in silence and ended in silence. No words came forth from the diamond cutter's mouth, but I heard them a thousand years later, a hundred *li* later north of the Silk Route in Genoa in a cave whose walls were covered in paintings of holy men who sang of silence, the desert-coloured silence, the yellow streams of silence, and blue, and white and fever. I went everywhere but arrived nowhere. I sat in perfect tranquillity, never left the cave, though I travelled ten-thousand leagues. The entire journey, all of it, a fever, a fever of appearance and delusion. I sat in perfect tranquillity. I never left the room, never left the cave, never heard the words, never said a thing. I should cut out my tongue, if I ever wake I'll cut out my tongue and throw it in the river in the ocean, in the lagoon, I'll chop it in bits and eat it. I'll feed it to Rusticello, hide it in his stew. He'll think he's died and gone to heaven. "There you have it, you have it all," I'll say. "You finally have it." But I won't say it because I won't have a tongue, so I'll sit in perfect tranquillity and look at him and open my mouth wide and watch the white lotus in my mouth shiver into red and I'll let him do all my speaking for me, let him wag on like an old gossip talking about this and that distant place, strange people all the bereft sadness of the world coming out of his mouth like an old sad tune, like the river flowing by, like the stars burning out, and I'll let him say all I couldn't say, wouldn't say, because the words weren't the end but just beginning and say, "Look!"

"I thought you were gone, my friend. Your babble never broke the surface, but I could see you were drowning in it, drowning in your memories." Rusticello offered him water in a chipped stoneware bowl.

Marco drank. "Despite the words you may have heard or not heard, all is silence there. In fact, nothing roars louder than the silence there. Whatever babble you might imagine, the silence is ever greater, and stronger and more vast."

"There is much more than mere words locked up in the fastness of your silence, my friend. Your heart constricts to the size of a hardened pea, and you refuse to see what is in front of you."

"So, at last you are giving up on me? Good. So be it." Marco handed back the empty bowl and collapsed back onto his pile of straw.

Later Rusticello said, "Man and wife could not be as intimate as we two have been these past months. We have watched each other piss and shit in the hole in the corner, shared each others' dreams, wept openly. And still you are a mystery to me. A hardness and a silence persist in your heart. Perhaps it is true of all Venetians, you men of the swamp and sea, you men who would rather count than measure. I don't know."

"And are all Pisans so taken with the sound of their own voices? I wonder."

Rusticello coughed into a rag, speckled with pink spots. "I would write it in blood if I could but find the words."

"Why don't you write your own story? Surely you have a story to tell?"

"Aaach, pray to tell, it would not be the same. My story is unimportant. My story is about recording your story. All my life has led to this moment, this chance. It is no coincidence that you and I have been thrown together here in this cell. If I were a woman I would have the tale out of you in a single night of passion."

"No doubt...no doubt," Marco nodded. "But, unfortunately, Rusticello, you are a man like me, and a hoary and crusty old one at that. No, you won't catch this bird with a net of passion."

"Riches?"

"No."

"Promises of eternal life? Dispensations? Indulgences?"

"Are you a priest then? You could no more make such promises than grow a womb." Marco laughed. "Like the bishops of Rome, you are a thoroughly unholy man."

"What then? What is your preferred temptation? Anything. I will give you anything."

Marco stared at him, said nothing.

"The stain on the ceiling appeared to me as an angel this morning. As I gazed at it, suddenly its wings flickered." Rusticello sat and stared at Marco who paced in the tight cell. "Imagine my surprise. I thought the angel had come to lead us out of here, or that I had died, or that it had some important message for me from the outside world."

"What, in the name of the Lord, could be important

enough to warrant the intercession of an angel to carry a message to you, a half-crazed Pisan? You are no Virgin large with child, of that I am sure. No, no, that belly of yours is not the result of child but the half-rotted onions and bad meat they have been feeding us these past months. You seem to thrive on it. I do not understand. While I waste toward nothingness, a mere skeleton under my hanging clothes, you retain your girth, your full cheeks, your fat priest's hands. That indeed is a miracle." Marco paused. "You know, Rusticello, I would give all my adventures, all my rich and half-forgotten memories, all my traveller's tales for a single plate of steaming mutton, a flagon of wine and a long night with Maria. No, my friend, the angel you saw was a mad dream come to mock us. We are forsaken. No one listens. Silence remains my only refuge, my comfort."

"And your worm."

Late that evening, the cellmates lay in darkness and silence. Out of the black, Marco spoke: "Rusticello. Sing to me. Sing one of your songs," and he did, letting the soft opalescent words rise into the dark air, letting them go, letting them vanish.

A spring breeze swirled the smell of rotting garbage and putrefaction into their cell. Rusticello, bowl held under chin, lifted a hunk of cold aubergine and pork fat with his fingers, and stuffed it into his mouth. Marco watched, his own bowl sitting on the floor.

"I cannot eat it."

"Suit yourself. I will have two bowls then– or do you prefer to leave it for the rats?"

"It is yours." Marco stared at the bowl, scratched at a flea.

"I have come to realize we are two very different types of men." Rusticello placed his empty bowl on the floor even as he eyed Marco's.

"Yes, no doubt," Marco said as Rusticello lifted the other bowl and continued shoveling the chunks of food into his maw, licking his fingers as he did so.

"Quite different."

"Unfortunately, I am a prisoner. I suppose there is no way I can escape hearing this."

"Mmm. No." Rusticello ran his tongue along the side of his hand. "I prefer to contemplate the world, then sing of its quiet joys, its sadness, its sweet light. You, on the other hand, prefer to experience the world—any momentary contemplation gets in the way of your next experience. But, in the end, I wonder if you truly experience anything at all."

Standing before the metallic mirror in the cell, Marco attempted to discern his face. He stood a long time trying to fix his own image, trying to see into the misty distance of the reflection.

In less than a year's time (it would be 1300), he would stand before another mirror, on one of the workshop islands of the Venetian lagoon, gazing into its depths, his beard trimmed, his wife and young child behind him in the open doorway of the glassworks. They would be speaking to the glassmaker, Salvatore Fiena, the one with the Saracen eyes and leathery skin.

"It is uncommonly clear," Marco would say to Salvatore in the mirror, and the image behind him would nod. "Not of metal but of glass, you say? A mirror of glass?"

"*Si*, it is the first. The idea came to me in a dream, a dream at dawn."

"It is said they are the true dreams," Marco's wife, Maria, would say, holding the hand of the little girl.

Marco would still be gazing into the mirror. "It is as if

you have taken the clearest stream, cut out a piece and stood it on end." Marco would reach out and touch the mirror with his finger to see that it did not ripple like water and, as he did so, he would notice that his finger fell on the column of the Lion of Venice, reflected from across the lagoon, the statue tiny and distant but clear as the man, woman and child standing in the open doorway. "It is...a wonder; yes, a wondrous thing you have done, Salvatore, a beautiful thing." Marco would turn from the mirror to face the glassmaker directly. "How many gold ducats will you take for it?"

Passion Play

I return to the city of my birth, as if back from the land of the dead. What could remain unchanged? I am a different man. Venice too must be different, a foreign city whose canals I somehow recall from a place out of time. And, after all this time, will he be waiting here as well?

For a year we sailed from island to island across black waters, following our Chinese mappa-mundi, *loading pepper, nutmeg, cloves, cubeb berries and galangal, heading for Zeilan, three thousand* li *across the southern seas. The soft breezes were scented with sandalwood and anise.*

Adim said the assassin would be there, in Zeilan, waiting for me when we arrived. I never saw him, but have no doubt he saw me.

Storms and disease thinned our numbers. We lost three ships in a typhoon that roared out of the Gulf of Siam. A month of fever filled the sea with bodies, until the ocean was gorged and appeased. Six hundred of our number died on the journey, though we Polos were somehow untouched.

In India, the heat was a kind of natural violence. It was there we heard of the Great Khan's death from other travellers. We delivered the princess to her fate, and Adim stayed to serve her. We parted in sadness, the dwarf and I.

We met traders in indigo, pepper and cinnamon; jewel merchants with diamonds sewn into their cloaks; and, once, a purveyor of birds, his line of camels dangling delicate wooden cages filled with kokatuas, luries, orange paroquets and bad-tempered peacocks, the bird that dreams its own tail.

And now this– a city of bright mist shimmering in the afternoon. Venice looks like a diamond in a swamp. Not an invisible city but a city made twice visible by the presence, on every hand, of water, the sea's water, breathing in and out of the canals. A city that exists in two places at one time, a city that surrounds you on every side, a city susceptible to weather, clouds rising at your feet, the sun glancing from a million places at once, the flash of night lightning multiplied at every turn. One city glittering with song; another dark with profound silence.

V*enezia*. Marco said the word to himself, trying out its sound on his tongue as he gazed at the city in the distance across the water.

The word sounded unusual coming from his own mouth. *Venezia*. What did it mean, this sound in a tongue now foreign to him, for his own language had grown rough with disuse over the years. Was he not a foreigner to this place? Or perhaps he had become a man without a land of his own. A perpetual traveller. The city continued to grow before his eyes as the ship cut through the water. Venice was coming back to him as he came back to it. A subtle echo of recognition, an empty mirror in his head filling up with a city.

As the ship neared Venice, the crew, pointing and jabbering, crowded the deck. Marco, his beard bushy and unkempt, was silent among them. His father and uncle stood nearby, sharing their thoughts quietly. They entered the scalloped waters of the lagoon, the winged Lion on its column sparkling in sunlight. Marco shifted his gaze to take in the rest of the city. He half-expected to see someone he knew hailing him from the small *sandolos* that came out to meet their ship. Marco, his father and uncle drew a few curious glances from the boatmen and others along the harbour, but in a city so frequented by exotic visitors, the Polos, with their faces only slightly more weatherbeaten than the average Venetian seaman, held but momentary interest.

When Marco placed his feet on the stones of Venice, an ineffable feeling arose in him. The city had existed as a patch of glittering gold light in his memory for so long it was as if a mirage hovering above the waters, out of nothingness, had come to life.

A short while later, when the Polos arrived at their house, they could hear a banquet in progress. Niccolo pounded on the door which was answered by a velvet-robed young man with thick black hair. "Who are you?" he asked. "We are celebrating a wedding feast. What is it you want?"

"This is my house," said Niccolo.

"What? Who are you, old man?"

"Tell the guests that Niccolo and Maffeo Polo have returned from the East, along with Marco, the son of Niccolo." Niccolo began to step through the doorway.

The young man put his open hand on Niccolo's chest to hold him back. "No, wait here."

Moments later, he returned. "They say you cannot be who you claim to be. The three Polos who travelled to the East must have died years ago. Nothing was ever heard from them. You must be beggars, or impersonators."

Marco stepped forward. "We have travelled far. Do not jest with us. Let us in." With Marco in the lead, the three of them stepped brusquely inside. *The smell*, thought Marco, *I remember the thick damp smell of this house.*

Passing through the ground floor storage room they mounted stairs to the next level and entered. The spacious rectangular room, its floor strewn with reeds, a bow hanging on the wall, was filled with guests seated at tables, drinking and laughing. *I recognize the faces, narrow, sculpted, pale, reserved. I recognize the intense, bulging eyes of the men; the softer lines of the women.* As the three strangers entered, an uncomfortable silence settled on the wedding guests.

"Who are you?" spoke a man with curly hair seated at the central table.

"Who are you?" Niccolo squinted. "Are you Stephano? Or perhaps Giovanni?"

From another table a tall grey-haired man said, "I am Giovanni," the crowd murmuring at the surprising revelation that the old stranger knew the names of some of their number.

Maffeo stepped forward and spoke. "Is Graziela here?"

A woman with wrinkles at the corners of her mouth said, "It is I."

"Do you not recognize me, wife?"

Graziela approached, wide-eyed, and touched Maffeo's face with a frail, angular hand. "Lord of angels, can it be true? I...I do not know. I am not sure. It is too long. I thought my husband was dead. I stopped thinking about him years ago, and his face slipped from my memory a few short months after he left. There is something in the voice, yes...but, I do not know for sure."

"Can you prove that you are the Polos?" said the one named Giovanni.

Niccolo proceeded to list the names of his many relatives, some of whom were present. Guests began nodding their heads and whispering among themselves. A few began arguing against this miracle.

"Let us send for others of our neighbours and see if any of them recognize you," said the young man who had answered the door. He sent two boys off to round up more distant relatives and the older of their neighbours.

"Offer the travellers a cup," someone in the crowd said.

The Polos dropped their bundles, accepted the cups and drank, as more relatives began to arrive from nearby, in wonder and awe at the possibility that the three could have returned.

"Who was Doge when you left?" asked Stephano.

"Lorenzo Tiepolo." Niccolo lowered his flagon of wine, as a ripple of surprise moved through the crowd surrounding the Polos. "And who is Doge now?"

"Pietro Gradenigo."

"Ah, a Gradenigo." Niccolo glanced at Maffeo who nodded.

"But two have since followed Tiepolo," said Giovanni. "Jacopo Contarini and Giovanni Dandolo."

"But, let us not disturb your festivities, you must go on with the wedding feast," Marco said to the assembled crowd, indicating the bride and groom. He stared at them as they sat at the main table, a young couple with fine skin and glowing faces. "And of the two, which is the Polo?"

A toothless crone, eyes glittering, spoke at his elbow. "Why, it is the groom. He is called Andreo Polo, the last son of your father's youngest brother, Tommaso, who died two winters ago." She paused. "But the bride has a sister, Maria. A girl of the age for marriage." She gestured to a young woman standing across the room by the wall.

Marco glanced at her, and she gazed back for a moment before turning away. In that momentary flash from her striking green eyes, he sensed a deep familiarity. He threw back his head and laughed.

In the middle of the night, Marco awakens and opens his eyes on the full moon hovering in his window. He hears the clear sound of footsteps approaching from a distance, hears them passing. He hears as he has not heard in years: a horse far off, clattering over a bridge of tarrred wood; the swish of a gondola as it slides along the canal, the small plash of its paddle, the gondolier's sigh; a woman weeping from several *cortes* away. For a moment, lying in the lonely timeless dark, he thinks he is a child and what he hears is his mother weeping as she sits on a step of their courtyard well. The clarity of the sound startles him. He rises from his bed, dresses and passes into the night.

Marco walks alone in the alleys and *cortes* of a sleeping city. He no longer hears the weeping. Nothing moves. All is still.

In moments, he is lost. Looking back the way he came to ensure no one follows, he takes an alley, crosses over a canal, walks along the *riva* next to the canal for a ways, turns into a covered lane. He wanders through the endless twists and turns of the place, the smells new and different as each bridge is crossed, the sounds echo more in one spot, are deadened in another. A gondolier passes down an eight-foot-wide canal, his head at the level of Marco's ankles, nods a greeting as he slips by and disappears around a turreted building.

The dark is unrelenting, though on a few squares torches burn in wall stanchions, scaring crazy shadows down nearby alleys.

The only sound his own footsteps, his own breath. Everything is compressed, he feels Venice inside himself, has always felt it there, though he barely recognizes it now, and yet there are echoes, smells, angles he recalls suddenly, like a detail remembered from a dream. The maze is compressing further and further until he feels the world has shrunk into this contorted city and the city has shrunk into a small bright point in his head.

Stopping on a bridge, he listens. He lets the silence sink into his bones, lets it come down inside him where it extinguishes all the exotic babble of the intervening years, as if washing him clean, emptying him.

Yes, against this silence I will remember all of it, each detail, each voice as it spoke, each trilling bird, each trickling chime, I will recall all of it, in high relief. He hears the lap-slap-lap in the canal under the bridge on which he stands. He sees stars rocking on the water, looks up and gazes into their bountiful silence.

The next night, the three travellers mounted a great feast to celebrate their return. Word had spread that the Polos had arrived home, everyone– cousins and uncles, neighbours and curious strangers–from nearby and distant quarters, came to see them.

In strict accordance with Mongol custom, the three Polos decided to carry out an elaborate ritual during the banquet. In the midst of the feast, when everyone was talking at once, drinking from flagons and munching on seafood and grapes mounded high on platters, the returned travellers rose from their seats at the long table, disappeared into an adjacent room and changed from robes of crimson satin into robes of crimson damask. On returning to the crowded banquet they cut up the satin robes and distributed the pieces to the assembled guests. Rough hands and fingers paused over the satin cloth, luxuriating in its richness.

The Polos answered endless questions with patience. Some in the crowd doubted the truth of their identity, but kept their doubts to themselves, in hopes of gaining some of the bounty. In a while, the Polos again mysteriously disappeared into the adjacent room. The guests waited in anticipation. The Polos returned in crimson robes of velvet, over their arms the damask robes which they distributed to select guests.

And again, after a while, they did the same with the velvet robes. The crowd buzzed at the wonder of this ritual. Marco, his father and uncle were enjoying the slow and deliberate ritual, elaborate as a passion play. They were finally dressed in their Venetian robes when Marco called to the servants, "Bring in our old travelling garments in which we first appeared."

"Things are not always as they seem," he said, as he slit the clothes open and dumped out onto the table handfuls of pearls, diamonds, sapphires, rubies and other gems. "Are these wonders real?" old Graziela asked Marco. He nodded. The Polos distributed a portion of the gems. The rest they gathered up for safekeeping in a sturdy wooden chest.

And with that, in answer to continuing questions from the guests, Marco began telling stories of their journeys. He did not notice that Niccolo and Maffeo at first stared down at the table in silent discomfort, then stole from the room as their relatives and neighbours crowded close.

A pallid light appears from the lagoon to the east. A breeze, silky and damp, lifts off the water with the rising dawn. Marco's tales have continued through the night. He is tireless, glowing with energy. Only the oldest and youngest among the guests have left. The rest are bewitched. "And in that way," Marco recounts, looking at their upturned faces, "we were able to escape the Muslims. For wrapped in slabs of pork on the wagon driven by the Christian– a Nestorian, he was– we knew we were safe from harm. The Muslims, as you know, have a profound distaste for pork. We knew they would not check the meat, and so we escaped beyond the walls of the town into the nearby hills where we bought mules and were on our way, riding all night and hiding in the day until we passed well beyond that country."

"And you kept the gold and jewels with you?"

"Yes. A meagre portion compared to what we had at the start. As you can see, we were wise to sew the jewels into our clothing, a ruse we learned from travelling merchants in India. A few other satchels of goods– mostly fine cloth– we were able to keep with us. Much else was lost. Ten times, a hundred times the value of what we brought back– which in itself is considerable– was left behind. Abandoned on the road. Paid out for food or horses or pack animals, or for safe passage through lands teeming with brigands."

"Still, you are wealthy men."

"Yes, it is true."

"And you have also the wealth of your stories. I think in the end they will prove more valuable than all your jewels," Maria says shyly.

He looks at her and smiles. "Yes, that too may be true."

Within days, the tales of Marco Polo had spread throughout the city, infiltrating every obscure alley, every secret square. In the evening, people would come to Marco wanting to hear it for themselves and he would tell them of the endless adventures and wonders that befell him on his journey east. The stories appeared like a mound rising in the midst of the compact sequestered city, rising higher and higher as he added more details, as he remembered and recounted events in Cathay, in Persia, in India and the southern islands. No one could ignore it– and soon word had passed along the rivers up into nearby towns and villages where the people treated the accounts like myths, or the embellished temptations of Satan.

"What think you?" a white-haired fisherman asked his friend as they unloaded baskets of blue-green squid onto the quay. "Is the younger Polo telling truths or not?"

"His father never traded in exaggerations when he returned before," said the other. "He stuck to jewels and cloth, the things he knew. As for me, I don't believe these tales. He says there are cities in Cathay ten, nay, twenty times the size of Venice, and life there is much like in Paradise. And the people act strangely, buying turtles and shellfish only to let them go back into the waters. He claims he saw palaces of gold and gems; huge birds that could lift a boat; savage people who run about naked and live on a milk that comes from the nuts of trees. I tell you, I think he suffers from a kind of madness, this Polo."

The first fisherman lifted the last basket of squid onto the dock. The large lidless eyes of the squid stared up into the sky. "If he speaks truth, my friend, I tell you this: it is the end of our world."

After watching a mystery play on the great square, my steps are traced in the night fog by one breathed up by the sea. At the moment I am about to slit the throat of my madness, the mist clears.

In front of the Church of San Marco, facing the piazza, workers had built a spacious platform to serve as a stage for the play, *The Mystery of Adam*, to be enacted that evening. A sizable crowd had gathered in the square and were avidly discussing the stage set. The floor of the platform was strewn with flowers, a number of bushes and plants had been set up, as well as trees bearing succulent fruits.

"Look at that," a man near Marco pointed to a tree at the rear of the stage, "one tree bears both apples and lemons." Those within earshot laughed, then went silent as the play began.

Out the doors of the church strode a white figure in a shimmering gold mask. He was immensely tall and his white robes seemed like snow on a mountainside. At centre stage he halted. Two angels came out leading Adam and Eve. Adam wore a red tunic, Eve a simple white dress. With flowers twined in their hair, they stood before God.

His voice thundered. "In the beginning God created Heaven and Earth. He created man in His own image and likeness."

A choir to the side chanted, "And the Lord God molded man of the dust of the ground, and breathed into his nostrils the spirit of life, and man became a living soul."

Adam and Eve stood with heads bowed. "This is your paradise." God's voice was strong but soothing. "You are to live here in happiness and joy, to delight in the green of the field, in the cavorting beasts, in the fruit of the earth." God motioned at the paradise set upon the stage, and stopped with his finger pointing at the tree in the centre. "But there exists one tree whose fruit you shall not eat."

What was it about the tree? Marco wondered as he stood watching with the crowd. Why was it there? *How is the garden of paradise different than heaven?*

At that moment, like dark thoughts flitting through the minds of Adam and Eve, a crowd of ragged demons scurried across a corner of the stage, up and then off. A moment later the half-dozen devils returned to hide behind the berry bush, unseen by the couple in paradise. Then they rushed out, a motley gaggle of horned beings, and startled Adam and Eve, encircling them, admiring their clothing, so rich in comparison to their own rags. The crowd gasped involuntarily as Satan appeared behind them, looking as tall and powerful as God himself (*Is it indeed the same player?* Marco wondered), but dressed in red and wearing a grotesque grimacing mask. He approached the couple.

Taking Adam by the hand, he leads him to the tree. Adam is powerless. Eve trails behind, peaking around Adam at the Devil. Satan picks a fruit, admires it and offers it to Adam who refuses it. He offers it again and Adam again refuses. Placing the apple in the crotch of the tree where two branches divide from the main trunk, Satan shows no anger but walks slowly off into the audience. The standing crowd divides as he passes, half in terror, half in delight. Satan appears to be thinking over his plan. As he wanders through the crowd, the pack of demons on stage watch with curiosity, as do Adam and Eve. Eve looks back at the apple. Satan sees her do this and slyly works his way back to the stage where he takes Eve gently by the hand and leads her to the tree. She quivers in fear but Satan strokes her arm and she begins to relax. Meanwhile, the demons have blindfolded poor Adam who is down on his hands and knees crawling in circles as they prod him and laugh. Satan and Eve have their backs to the audience. When they turn about she holds the apple in the cup of her hands, her arms held straight out before her. She appears stunned, staring at it in disbelief. The apple glows with an impossible redness as if it were alive and pulsating. Satan smiles broadly, calls to his pack and they exit the stage, climbing down beneath it where they send up an otherworldly wailing. Eve remains frozen, staring at the apple. Adam has fallen asleep on his belly, still blindfolded.

After God banished Adam and Eve from paradise, the devils cavorted about the stage, banging on iron pans as they placed the couple in chains and fetters. Marco noted that the crowd seemed to enjoy this display more than any other. The play ended with Adam and Eve being hauled down to hell under the stage from where smoke trailed out into the evening air.

The crowd began to drift away. Marco stayed back to talk in the square with friends. A mist of quiet settled on the city.

In mottled dusk, Marco takes his leave and slips into a narrow street at the far side of the piazza. Fog, crawling up out of the sea and tasting of salt, sends its soft colourless tendrils down lost alleys and slick cloacal waterways. A pair of disembodied heads appears out of mist and slips back into it, voices muffled and echoing from unexpected places. Ghosts. Voices of ghosts.

Marco walks for a while, turns, looks back. Hears behind him light footfalls that stop when he stops, start when he starts. The gauzy fog so thick he cannot tell if night has already fallen or if dusk is yet drifting into the creviced alleyways.

He walks on. Stops again. Hears a sound behind him and wraps his hand around the haft of the knife under his shirt. He walks on, a little faster.

From a stone bridge he hears the *slap slap* of black water. A gondola slides by into silence.

"Who goes there?" His own voice. It sounds overly loud but is swallowed a few feet from him.

He spots a figure half-immersed in fog, a single eye, a horn protruding at an angle from the forehead above it. Then nothing.

A demon then. I am traced by a demon. Is it him? Is it him at long last? He fights an urge to flee.

"What is it you want?" His shout dies in the mist. Turning, he walks on, not quickly but at a steady pace, hand gripping his knife.

In his home *corte*, a torch flickers in an iron wall stanchion rimed with salt. He sees the familiar well at the center of the courtyard and walks to it.

He halts. Looks behind, sees nothing. Gazes down into the impenetrable dark of the well.

The blackness. The same blackness I saw when I was a boy, when I stood here with my aunt and met my father for the first time.

When he looks up, a demon from the play stands on the far side of the well, staring at him. A pair of horns protruding from its forehead, a grotesque face with a mouth frozen in a scream, a long hairless tail.

"What do you want?"

The devil says nothing, continues staring. Marco walks around the well. As he does so, the demon too moves around the well, keeping its distance.

"Why have you followed me?"

Marco approaches again and the demon retreats. He stares at the figure. *It must be him, come to confront me at last– but why does he not speak?*

"Speak!"

The demon stares at him, turns and flees into the mist.

He waits in the fog and dark. *He is teasing me– trying to heighten my fear.*

He stands by the well with the patience of a fisherman checking his octopus pots. As he waits, the arms of the mist embrace him.

Late in the heart of the night, he looks into the well again– and, when he looks up, the demon is staring at him.

Marco tries to approach and, as before, the other keeps its distance on the far side of the well. The knife is in his hand, under his shirt, near his pounding heart.

From across the small square they hear the sound of

someone passing. The devil quickly turns and disappears in the fog.

Again Marco waits, for hours and, with a start, realizes he has been gazing thoughtlessly into the well, gazing down into its unfathomable sleep, its blank dream, that seems to connect in some deep place with all other wells, all other sleeps and dreams.

Near dawn, he wakes, looks up and sees the devil staring at him as before.

"Why do you torture me? You have dogged me for years, burdened my sleeps, haunted my days. Your mouth is frozen in a scream yet no sounds come forth from you."

The demon tilts its head to the side, and slowly lowers its gaze.

A long tense silence pours out of the night all around them. Behind the devil the torch on the wall gutters and throws a spark, and with that Marco leaps across the well and tumbles the demon to the ground, the knife instantly at the devil's throat.

"Wait." A woman's voice, not a man's.

The knife falls from his hand and clatters on the cobbles. Now that he is close he can see, staring at him from behind the mask, her green eyes.

A messenger summoned Marco to the chambers of Giorgio Contarini, his boyhood friend, who had risen to a position of considerable importance as a Franciscan prelate. Marco walked across the Campo di Santa Margherita, stepped under a stone archway and entered a circumscribed court-yard paved with stones in a herringbone pattern. As he crossed the shadow of the threshold, Marco noticed a small woman sitting on a step at the foot of a well. When she looked up, it appeared as if she had been waiting for him. She stood and ambled over on her unnaturally short legs. The dwarf had long, straggly, greasy black and grey hair and wore a shift that was little more than a rag. Her enormous eyes bulged out of her head.

"Come in, come in," she said in a high sing-song voice that instantly told Marco she was mad. "Let me look at you. The Virgin preserve us, I know you, the Greek-tongued Lucifer! Tongue of the Devil!" She tilted her head. "I know you. *Mentitore*, liar, the mad one they call you! *Fantastico!* Mad! You! *Si, si*, it is true, the truth of God and angels, but your tongue is black, it's black! *Signore lingua nera bocca nera, si si, falso mendace bugiardo sbagliato favoloso favolatore, lingua di favolatore....*"

Marco backed to the stone stairs in a corner of the court-yard as she cursed at him, spitting as she shouted.

Giorgio heard the commotion and came to the head of the stairs. "Ignore her, Marco. She is a madwoman, but harmless."

Marco hurried up the stairs and with an embrace greeted Giorgio who wore a long grey tunic with a white cord at the waist. After passing through the parlatory, reserved for receiving non-clerical visitors of lesser importance, they entered the priest's private chambers.

The room was dark and had little furniture: a few chairs, a writing desk. One wall held an ominous crucifix with a blood-splattered Christ.

After the formalities were disposed of, Marco said, "I hear you are a man of much power now, Giorgio. You have come far from the young novice I once knew."

"Yes, I do not deny it." Giorgio took pride in the fact.

Power rested comfortably on his wide shoulders. He sat straight in his hard chair, an unspoken resistance turning every smile into a sneer. "But all my powers are ultimately in the service of God."

"Of course. But why is it you have sent a messenger to summon me? I would have come to visit in a few days more, in any case, but now I have the excuse to come sooner. Tell me, dear friend, why have you sent for me?"

"Yes, Marco. To the point. It is these...tales...you are disseminating throughout the city. Oh, yes, word travels fast, especially when such fabulous notions are put about. The people are in a fever of imagination over it. You must desist, Marco. I urge you to cease telling these lies which inflame the congregations."

"Lies? These are no lies! I am telling what I have seen with my own eyes or what others have told me." Marco leapt up and went to the window, stared out with his back to the other. "There is much I have not yet revealed of those astonishing lands. I do *not* tell lies."

Giorgio held up his hand, palm out. "Please. Be calm. Aquinas teaches us to beware the innate dangers of travel taken for the sake of *curiositas* rather than *pietas*. Your travels were certainly no pilgrimage, I am sure of that. You might ask yourself, Marco, what it is about your tales that disturbs our people. Surely it is not that the stories are marvellous. These people feast on the marvellous. It is your claim that these tales are true. True! Are you mad that you claim they be true?"

Marco heard the door behind him open. Another friar entered. He barely glanced at Marco's back before whispering in Giorgio's ear. *That voice!* A cold light pricked Marco's heart. He swung about and saw before him the wiry form of the bitter-faced assassin. He turned back to the window, stared at his hands and held his breath. The monk consulted with Giorgio, then left the room.

Giorgio continued. "You might believe you have seen and experienced such things but it is my contention that you have been misled by demons. I believe you have been, in a way, possessed. And because you have become a vessel of the Devil's, you see the truth as lies and lies as truth. Is it not so?"

"Is this an inquisition? Am I to be doubted by my oldest friend?"

"Please, do not disturb yourself. This is not an inquisition and I do not believe you have acted with malice in your heart. But I do believe– and I have spent much time in prayer over this vexatious question– I do believe you have been duped, tricked by evil powers who wish to use you for their own purposes. The Devil works in many subtle ways. I only ask you to be silent, to cease telling these outrageous stories. Is that so much?"

Marco turned and looked out the window. The still air hung heavily, dirty clouds had gathered over the city, as if a storm were about to break. Giorgio awaited a response. Marco walked to the door and without glancing back, left.

I watch her come and go from her house. I am hidden in the shadows. I don't know what draws me here, only that I must follow the promptings of my heart.

The thin, perfectly round, gold bracelet sat on the smooth stone of the doorstep. Marco watched patiently from the shadows of a covered walkway across the narrow canal.

Next to the door, a flowerbox below a window spilled vines of red flowers in the early morning sunlight.

She came to the door, stood looking out on the new day, a brown and white cat luxuriating in her arms. Maria's green eyes searched the morning sky between houses, as she stroked the cat, nuzzling under its chin, rubbing its ears. Marco could see the blondish hairs of her bare forearms.

As she turned to go back into the house she stopped short, having noticed the bracelet on the doorstep. Quizzically, she bent down, letting the cat flow from her arms and picked up the bracelet. She turned it in her fingers, then smiled to herself and slipped it on. She admired it a moment, took one more glance about the empty courtyard and turned back into the house.

The next morning, in the same place, she found a bracelet of finely entwined silver rings thin as horsehairs. And the morning after, one with tiny gold bells. Each morning, she added them, one by one, to her arms– bracelets of jade, lapis lazuli, mother of pearl.

On the twelfth morning, she found one of twisted gold holding a fine scroll of parchment– a note Marco had paid a local scribe to write for him.

"This eve, when the sun is about to empty its shining heart into the sea, meet me on the stone bench beneath the tree on Campo Santa Margherita. Marco Polo."

Maria wondered at the boldness of the note, but was also intrigued by it. *Perhaps this strange ritual is something done in the East. Perhaps he never learned our complex rules of courting. Of course, it was forward of me to follow him to the well.* She rubbed the bracelet along her cheek and slipped it on.

When she arrived at the Campo that evening, Marco was waiting on the bench. Maria walked to him, took his hand in silence, looked into his eyes and, before he could speak, leaned forward and whispered in his ear.

On a glorious day in spring I wed Maria of the green eyes. Thousands attend the ceremony in the glittering depths of San Marco. I am so elated, so weightless with joy, that I hear as I have never heard before: the sound of a feather falling on an island in the distance; the sound of sunlight warming the cobbles of the piazza; light penetrating the green waters of the lagoon. My relatives tell us that our faces are radiant and our eyes shine. Even the sight of the assassin watching from the high reaches of the church cannot stain this day.

The bold brown and white cat, its tail and nose in the air, strutted through the doorway, sniffing. Neither Maria nor Marco saw it, for they had their backs to the door as they inspected the long hake frowning on the wooden table. The cat paused, realizing its path to the fish would have to be slightly more circuitous than anticipated.

"Is it big enough?"

"I'm not sure." Maria, holding a cleaver in her left hand, flipped the fish over. "It's thin. How many will we be?"

Marco ignored her question and nuzzled her neck and hair, which smelled of rosemary. As she turned to him, the cat timed its leap with perfection, snatched the fish in its mouth and made for the door.

"Stop him!" shouted Maria.

Marco leapt after the cat, grabbing its tail for a moment before it slipped free and shot down the stairs, Marco and Maria in pursuit.

"Stop him!" she shouted again.

"I'm trying to," Marco cried over his shoulder.

At the bottom of the stairs, the cat realized the door to outside was shut, turned instantly, shooting between Maria's legs, whacking her ankles with the head and tail of the fish, and fled back up the stairs, the others again in pursuit.

Maria still had the cleaver in hand and when old Niccolo saw them in the hall, he surmised, quite logically, that she was attempting to plant the fish-cutting implement into the back of Marco's neck.

"Maria!" he shouted. *"Alto!"*

"I'll kill him!" she stormed.

"My only son! So soon after the wedding!" Niccolo limped along the hall. *"Dio mio. Alto!"*

Meanwhile, the cat had scurried under a table and along the wall, knocking over small barrels and jugs with the fish as it ran. Dried peas trickled across the floor.

"Where is it? Do you see it?" Marco asked Maria. They turned in circles in the center of the room. Niccolo stood in the doorway, weeping, "Maria, Maria, do not do this thing."

"There it is!" Marco leapt for the cat as it slipped by Niccolo and out the door again, the fish still clutched in its jaws. The cat, not one to repeat its mistakes, this time made down the hall where it found an open window and escaped. Marco watched, cursing, as it fled down the alley, the tail of its prize flapping in the breeze.

Back in the kitchen, Maria raised the cleaver high over her head and sunk it an inch deep in the wood of the table. "Now look what you've done."

Niccolo bowed his head. "I thought you were going to kill Marco."

She turned around, smiling, and shook her head.

Marco stood looking from the second-story window at the boats moving along the sparkling waters of the Grand

Canal. "How can this be? So soon?"

Maria sat on a divan, her head bowed. "Two months have passed since the wedding. Long enough. It is a sign, I think, Marco, a sign that we are meant in this world for one another."

"Yes. Sometimes I think I came back from the East, without knowing it, for you and you alone. For nothing else. And now this. A child. I am very happy."

Sitting on the square with a small group of friends, Marco pours round another pot of wine.

"And did this truly happen, Marco, this tale of the carpet-maker of Kierman, or is it a story you have invented for our entertainment? You know the people are calling you *Marco Milione* for your exaggerations. Did these things truly happen?"

"I know what I have seen, my friends. I know what I have experienced. But I tell you this— we live a tale every day, a story of our own invention, that is what I have learned from the storytellers, from the carpet-maker, from Rashid, from Adim and others."

He could sense that the faces of his friends began to darken with doubt. Only Maria was with him, and she smiled sadly from across the table. In the awkward silence that followed, Marco felt pierced by a loneliness of an order utterly different than that found on the empty wastes of desert or plain.

I begin to see that my tales, offered only as entertainment and a source of knowledge about the wide world— certainly

not the teachings of wisdom– have disturbed the people of Venice. Their hearts and minds are in a ferment. This was not my intention. I grow isolated now, alone with my dreams and memories. It is not the world I imagined for my wife and child.

"My good Christians and fellow Venetians, it is said that the angels are the pure messengers of God. But if you believe in angels, as you must, for men have seen them all about us, you must also take note of the presence of devils in our midst, devils who whisper lies and deceit in the ears of God-fearing men and women." Giorgio's voice boomed from the raised pulpit. Marco, with Maria and baby Anna, had filed into crowded San Marco on the feast of the Ascension, carrying their stools which they set down on the stone floor. Marco stared at his boyhood friend and marvelled as he stood above the congregation, his voice resonant, his chest swelled, his mouth arced in a permanent frown.

A dozen acolytes swung censers that puffed out clouds of thick roiling incense. The church filled with the sickly sweet fog. The clouds drifted up into the towering domes of the church, muting the brilliance of the mosaics.

Giorgio preached, his strong voice filled with authority and conviction. "Let me read to you now from the Book of Revelations of St. John:

> *And round about the throne were four and twenty seats, and upon the seats I saw four and twenty elders sitting, clothed in white raiment, and they had on their heads crowns of gold.*
> *And out of the throne proceeded lightnings and thunderings and voices, and there were seven lamps of fire burning before the throne, which are the seven Spirits of God.*

And before the throne there was a sea of glass like unto crystal, and in the midst of the throne, and round about the throne, were four beasts full of eyes before and behind.

And the first beast was like a lion, and the second beast was like a calf, and the third beast had a face as a man, and the fourth beast was like a flying eagle.

And the four beasts had each of them six wings about him; and they were full of eyes within....

"And I repeat: *full of eyes before and behind, and they were full of eyes within....*And so must we be, with our eyes looking in every direction, forward, backward and even within, for the Beast is everywhere among us ready to rob us of our souls, the Beast clothed in the cloth of our neighbours and friends, the Beast in our midst. And even as Angels are the bearers of good tidings, so too are there evil messengers, the willing messengers of Satan, those who would deliver the message of un-godly beliefs, of foreign ways, of distant pagan teachings."

Marco felt as if Giorgio had picked him out of the congregation and was staring at him. He began to feel that others in the church knew who the priest was speaking of and many turned to stare, boldly or surreptitiously, at him and his family, for he was easily recognized by the citizens of the city.

"We must learn to block up our ears, to block up the mouths of those who speak such untruths, such outrageous exaggerations and lies, for they are indeed lies, every one; they go against the teachings of Christ the God, the very word of God, for they are a calumny hidden in the fascinations of the new and exotic and different. They are calumny for they slander God himself. Let us silence them in any way we can for they come to destroy the earth and all good Christians upon it, they are Satan come to earth in human form just as Christ came to us as a man. Let us not doubt for a moment that Satan has power, endless resources at his behest and will use them in any way possible to steal souls to people his infernal regions. Though Lucifer be frozen upside down in ice in the deepest depths of Hell, he sees much and he knows much. He reaches out in the form of his minions to grab us about the throat and swallow us into his evil. To know too much is an evil thing–leave knowledge to the priests who know what to do with it. Leave the fine distinctions between *quod est* and *quo est* to those of us who have studied the mind of God and understand the language of the Popes."

Marco looked at the blank faces about him as Giorgio continued in the private and priestly language. Neither Marco nor any of his neighbours understood Latin. When he had finished speaking a few lines, he continued with the sermon.

"I *demand* that the people of Venice take it upon themselves to rid the city of this vermin, the beasts that bring back the seed of the unholy from distant places, the exaggerations of hellish paradises, the lies from over the seas." Giorgio lifted his fists in the air, sharpened and raised his voice, his brows knitting together with intensity, his face severe and hard. "All is justified, all is demanded. We must cleanse ourselves, cleanse our city of such unholy filth, or we will be dragged down into the lair of demons, there to suffer eternal damnation, eternal degradation, eternal suffering beyond the rescue of God or His saints. Act now, or face eternal damnation. Amen."

When the mass was finished and Marco and his family

were exiting the church, the crowd kept its distance. Marco heard whispers, but kept his head down and, holding his stool in his hand, left the church for the piazza. Maria, her eyes proud and defiant, walked by his side holding Anna.

In the capacious square, stalls had been set out for the Ascension Day fair but Marco and his family hardly looked at the booths displaying wares from all over Europe. Venetian merchants haggled with traders from Pisa, Florence and Milan, from France, Spain and Germany. But Marco and Maria walked briskly through the square in silence seeking the haven of their home quarter.

As they walked, Marco thought about the invitation to join the Doge later that day on his gilded barque, the Bucintoro, for the ritual Ascension Day ceremony.

Surrounded by hundreds of lesser craft, the Doge's golden barge eased through the port of San Nicolo and headed through scalloped waters for the open sea. Forty-two elegant painted oars dipping rhythmically in the brilliant waters propelled the two-storey ceremonial ship of state. The Doge's parasol was mounted on the prow and a golden winged lion, rampant, guarded the stern. The barque was a floating drawing room, the long assembly hall lined with benches where now sat all the wealth and power of Venice in their best robes of gold, silver or blue. They conversed in small groups, gesturing at the fineness of the day.

At the head of the assembly hall, a great goddess held a sword and balancing pans. The figure of Neptune stood near two winged cherubs, an empty suit of armor and, high on the prow, four gods of wind with carved gusts sweeping from their perfectly circled mouths. Swirling above in a sun-swollen sky, grey and white gulls turned in endless complaint.

Marco breathed the salt breeze and was surprised to feel

himself shiver with pride at being a free man of the great city of Venice. The memory of Cathay was slipping inexorably away. Nearby him stood Niccolo and Maffeo looking august in their finery, but still lean and stiff as weatherbeaten masts wrapped in sail cloth.

A single cry went up and the oarsmen, in elegant livery, raised the oars out of the water. The great ship bobbed in the vastness of open sea as hundreds of smaller boats gathered behind. The Patriarch of Venice, his clerical robes flickering in the breeze, his mitre standing tall on his head, walked to the prow and ceremoniously emptied a cruet of holy water into the sea, raised his hands high and declaimed to the assembled multitude:

*Keep safe from stormy weather, Oh Lord, all
your faithful mariners,
safe from sudden shipwreck and from evil,
unsuspected tricks of cunning enemies.*

Next to the Patriarch, Doge Pietro Gradenigo, his lined face like a peach stone topping robes of golden silk, passed his hand over the seas. From a pillow held by a retainer on his left, he took the golden ring in his fingers, raised it high where it circled the sun and flung it with a flourish into the waves. Once again Venice was "married" to the sea. The crowds burst into cheers and chanted: *Pax tibi Marce Evangelista meus!* and *Viva San Marco!* Thousands of white flowers filled the air and littered the waters, sending the gulls into a frenzy.

During the return journey, a guard led Marco to his audience with the Doge. Marco went down on one knee and then was given a seat. The retainers and servants backed away to allow a private conversation.

"As you know, Marco Polo, our ships will soon be leaving for battle against Genoa. We suspect we will confront the Genoese fleet before too long. I would like you to accept a commission as a Gentleman Commander." The Doge held up his hand before Marco could speak. "Let me be frank. I have much admiration for you and your family, but there are many here who are less than happy with your successes. Call it ancient antagonisms, or perhaps jealousy. I don't know. In any case there is little I can do about it. Perhaps if you were to distinguish yourself in battle, it would be help-ful. This much I do know: it would be an auspicious time for you to leave."

"And my father, my uncle?"

"Because they are old, they no longer pose a threat to anyone. They are safe. But you, Marco Polo, have caught the notice of too many eyes and ears. Your tales are believed by some and feared by others. I, for one, know not what to make of them, although I know all things are possible in this world. At any rate, I wish you well. Godspeed."

I see where all my storytelling leads. At last I confront him. I am speechless.

Preceded by a distant churning of voices, the animated crowd echoed as it approached the square through a constricted alley.

Marco glanced up in the direction of the sound. He and Niccolo were taking the evening sun in the wide square near the Polo palazzo. On stone benches under a wall lit sienna, they sat talking to a few of Niccolo's old friends and drinking *vino nero* from tankards. Marco had been telling them of his selection as a Gentleman Commander.

"When will the ships leave?" Niccolo asked sadly.

"I don't know. Soon."

Three- and four-story houses of muted tangerine or powdery apricot circled the square, the colours of the houses so dusted by the slow passage of time that they blended and harmonized perfectly. Two old shapely trees, not large but voluptuously curved, completed the tableau.

Marco noticed how his father had aged since their return, touched by the alchemy of time, his hair gone white, his eyes a weak yellow, his skin thin and mottled as hammered silver.

"What are they shouting?" The old man leaned forward as the crowd, loud and dissonant, spilled into the far end of the *campo*.

Tilting his head, Marco listened.

"*Dio mio!*" He leapt up, grabbed the startled Niccolo by the arm, hurried him down a nearby *calle*, over a stepped bridge and into a doorway cut in the wall.

Once inside, Marco latched and bolted the heavy door while Niccolo waited.

"What is it? What are they shouting?"

"They shout, '*Marco Milione, diavolo, demonio!*'"

"Aieee! Let us get our swords and gather the servants!"

Upstairs, Maffeo, Graziela, and Maria, with the child in her arms, rushed to the door. "What is it? We heard the crowd."

As Marco hurried to the window overlooking the square, Niccolo said, "They are calling him *Marco Milione*. Jealous ignorant fools!"

Marco looked down into the *corte*. About two dozen

young men, several well-known troublemakers among them, had gathered below, shouting and shaking their fists. His eyes searched the square for the assassin but he was nowhere to be seen.

"There he is! *Marco Milione!*" someone cried out below and a rock cracked against the palazzo wall beside the window, followed by a hail of shouts. Around the square, doorways filled with people who had heard the commotion. Some yelled at the mob to desist and go home, a few others joined in. After a bit more shouting the crowd's energy descended into mumbles and half-hearted complaint. Small groups broke off and drifted into the descending dark, leaving the square silent and empty, but for one of their number sprawled out drunk on the cobbles.

Marco unclipped his sword and dropped into a chair.

Out of the heavy silence, Maffeo spoke. "They say the Great Council has met to discuss how your tales have disturbed order in the city. Some are saying we will be called before the Doge." He placed his arm around his wife who whimpered into her hands.

Niccolo looked at his son. "What say you now, Marco? You see why I ceased speaking of my travels when I returned from the East the first time? Do you see what folly it is?"

Marco bowed his head.

Late that night, Marco threads his way through the solidified dark of the city. He follows deserted alleys until he enters into Piazza San Marco, and hurries unseen across it to the Molo at the edge of the lagoon. The restless mephitic water shifts back and forth, smelling of fish and seaweed. The walls of the square seem to close in. He is caught and can hardly breathe. As he takes the small box of soil from his pocket and slides it open he can feel the attention of the winged Lion at his back. Marco pauses.

Gritting his teeth, he flicks the soil across the water, flinging the box after.

He hears the sound of a breath behind him and turns. The assassin stands ten paces away, his dull eyes staring without emotion.

"At last we meet." Marco bows slightly. The other remains still and says nothing.

The assassin suddenly rushes at Marco and knocks him down. A stilleto flashes and catches Marco in the palm, pinning his left hand against the cobbles. He stifles a scream for he does not want the Doge's night guards to come running. He does not want the struggle stopped. He knows their confrontation must come to an end this night. The assassin tugs his knife out of Marco's hand and in that moment Marco lunges up with all his strength, slamming his shoulder into the other's chest. The friar loses balance, goes tumbling backwards and slams the back of his skull into the column of the winged Lion. Immediately his skull is crushed.

The assassin slumps to the cobbles and Marco approaches, holding his injured hand against his chest. A trickle of blood oozes from the dead man's mouth, his eyes wide. Marco sees something on the ground at his feet and bends down to pick it up. With a start he realizes what he holds in his hand– the assassin's severed tongue.

He looks up into a sky full of glistening stars. No sound but the water slapping the wall. Marco stares a long while. Out of the clear sky he feels a drop of rain on his face, slow rain, dark and rich as ink, sparkling, gold-rimmed, floating down like seeds out of the opulent black night.

A Jail Cell In Genoa (VI)

Turning in the fifty-five cosmological spheres of my dreams, I am lost in wondrous tales, travelling on and on, beyond, and beyond the beyond, to the end.

Rusticello stared out the window at the night sky over Genoa. He pondered the string of stars in Orion's belt. "Let me say this, for I believe I have come to know you a little." He turned around to look at Marco and spread his arms wide. "The Venetians are a supremely practical people– they think the stars exist merely for navigation and nothing else. But Marco, you are different. Stop pretending you are nothing but a man of adventure. You only announce this in order to hide behind it. Stop clinging to your silence like a mollusk. Of course there will be those who are jealous of your experiences, jealous of whatever joys you have wrung from this life. Let them dry up in their jealousy like grapes left too long on the vine. Ignore their bitter taunts. Do what you must. I and all the angels of heaven beseech you; speak out, before you drive me mad at the sound of my own voice."

"That would make two of us."

Marco smiled broadly at Rusticello, and turned his face to the cell door as the other went back to staring at the night sky.

Rusticello spoke quietly. "Aristotle the Greek posited fifty-five cosmological spheres in the heavens. I am reminded of the domes and cupolas of Chiesa San Marco, like Chinese nesting bowls. But here the stars are distant– out of reach, out of earshot. Here they have no desire to hear our songs. They seem hard. Brilliant but uninterested."

With the first light, Rusticello stood from his pile of straw and, as he stretched and yawned, noticed the bottle of ink on the shelf. "How odd." He reached for the bottle, uncorked it and stuck his finger in. "Look. The ink. It is moist again."

Taking the bottle, Marco looked in. "Yes. Something has quickened it." He lifted it to his nostrils and a conflux of odours drifted out: the smell of night rain, lush jungle mist, camel dung, sandalwood and rose perfume, the smell of live turtles in Hangchow, of lemons in Persia, of fires from the ghats of Maabar, the smell of leather and dust, mountain streams and hot resinous trees, musk and sweat and steaming rice wine.

Marco stuck his finger into the ink and stirred, withdrew his finger and licked it, recognizing a taste familiar yet unnameable.

From his straw pile, Marco glanced up at a distant sound, a long run of tumbling thunder. "A storm comes."

He handed the bottle back to Rusticello who, like a priest, held it aloft and bowed. As he placed the bottle of ink back on its shelf, the smaller door inside the large door to their cell slid open and a hand came through holding a bowl. The voice behind the hand grunted.

Rusticello took the bowl and offered it to Marco. Another bowl appeared which the Pisan took for himself.

They sit on their piles of straw and eat in silence. Outside, below the thunder, a pair of melodious warblers still call to each other while the sun's voice shines. Marco glances out. "Black clouds." In that moment the sun is blotted out and the birds fall silent. Streaks of rain appear out of the sky. Marco turns back to his food.

"This soup– what is in it?"

"I don't know."

They continue spooning the thick slop into their mouths while the rain begins to drive hard, whipped by the wind. With a flash, lightning writes across the sky and thunder drums. Rusticello is still looking out the window when Marco leaps up, knocking his bowl to the floor. Rusticello watches it roll across the room.

A massive and peculiar silence descends, penetrating every crevice of their cell, the thunder too as if holding its breath. A confused look crosses Rusticello's face.

"What? What is it?"

Marco's hands are gripped into fists at his sides as he drops to his knees before the door. He clutches at his throat, tears at it in terrifying inescapable silence.

"What is it!?" Rusticello leaps to his feet as Marco turns red then purple then white, his teeth locked together.

Finally Rusticello understands. He begins pounding on Marco's back but that has no effect. He grabs Marco's hair and smashes his forehead and face into the door. Over and over Rusticello, grunting with effort, bangs the skull into the heavy wood with a dull flat thud. He can feel Marco going limp in his hands. Rusticello slams the head again, with all his strength, into the wood of the unyielding door. Again and again, beyond hope, he smashes the head and shouts, "Let it go! Let it go!"

With a strangulated wail, Marco's throat spits forth a piece of bone which falls to the floor. He collapses onto his back, face bruised and blood dripping from his nose and lips. He stares at the ceiling, mumbling, "My God, my God."

Rusticello sighs and wipes sweat from his face, picks up the piece of bone, places it in the palm of his hand and stares at the drum-shaped vertebra. He kneels behind

Marco, takes his head in his hands.

Marco, amazed, sees the door to their cell blow open, the viscid black water of a canal lapping at the door sill, rain driving hard, a thousand distant voices rising ceaselessly from the depths of the waves. He sees the winged Lion stare down at them, its eyes glowing white. Black storm clouds roil and churn and lightning splinters the heavens behind its head.

The sides of the Lion distend with each breath. Its muscles quiver as if it is about to leap.

The Lion roars, flushes white from its glowing eyes outward, across its face and along its flanks, turning pure alpha white to the tips of its shimmering wings. The beast begins to flow down in a spasm of radiance, spirals down into Marco like an uncoiled umbilicus of white rope falling from the sky.

Rusticello is already reaching for the bottle of ink as Marco begins to speak.

Acknowledgments

While this is a work of fiction almost all the characters once lived and breathed on this earth. A few– Rashid, Adim, Gesualdo, Giorgio and others– were born in the realm of the imagination. But who can say that they never lived, long ago, in those distant lands?

About eighty-five early manuscripts of Marco Polo's travels are preserved in various libraries and museums. They are written in Italian, Latin or French and no two are exactly alike. The earliest extant versions are from the mid-1500's. I consulted two versions for this work: *The Travels of Marco Polo (The Venetian)* from Boni and Liveright, based on the classical English version from the nineteenth century by Marsden. I also used *Marco Polo, Travels*, which included extremely helpful footnotes and was published by Everyman's Library.

Another work, which served as a primary inspiration, bears the same title as this one. *The Lion of Venice*, subtitled *Studies and Research on the Bronze Statue in the Piazzetta*, was edited by Bianca Maria Scarfi and was published as an accompaniment to exhibitions of the statue of the Lion in England and Italy. This beautiful book brought the Lion to life for me, and provided the first spark of the creature that breathes here.

It would be impossible to mention all the works consulted, but several demand recognition for their inspiration and their assistance. John Julius Norwich's *A History of Venice* was invaluable as was *Venice, A Maritime Republic* by

Frederic Lane. Also, *Baedeker's Venice* as well as James (now Jan) Morris's incomparable *Venice*, were extremely helpful and always a joy to read and consult.

The information on mulberry trees, silk moths and silk production, as well as many other details about China, were found in *Science and Civilisation in China*, Joseph Needham's masterpiece, a multi-volume work which is a Borgesian world of its own.

The murder scene in the Venetian Arsenal was inspired by a few lines from Dante's *Inferno, Canto XXI*, in which he compares hell's pitch to that of the Arsenal, bubbling "not by fire but by divine art."

Information on Provencal romances and ballads came from *The Complete Romances of Chretien de Troyes* by David Staines.

The section in which Rashid performs a geomantic divination in the sand was inspired by Volume 13 of *Alaeddin and the Enchanted Lamp*, "done into English from the recently discovered Arabic text" by John Payne, Khorassan edition (1901).

Many works on Tartar, Persian and Chinese history and Yuan drama were also consulted and are too numerous to mention. I have the screenplay of Kurosawa's *Seven Samurai* to thank for suggesting the choreography in several of the jail scenes in Genoa.

Other works which were important, sometimes in a tangential way, were: *A Year Amongst the Persians* by Edward Browne; *In Xanadu: A Quest* by William Dalrymple; *The Bulfinch Guide to Carpets* by Enza Milanesi, a lovely and fascinating book; Michael Marqusee's *Venice: An Illustrated Anthology*; and *Venice, A Portable Reader* by Toby Cole which includes an absolutely stirring account of Casanova's escape from the Doge's prison. And thanks to Jeff Street,

Henry Chapin and Nicola Vulpe for providing helpful books at various times during the research. Needless to say, any errors of fact that have occurred are solely my own.

I would like to acknowledge the Ontario Arts Council for a Works-in-Progress grant during the writing of this book. Also, an early version of the first section appeared in *Paper Guitar*, edited by Karen Mulhallen and published by HarperCollins (Toronto, 1995).

I also would like to thank my agent, Jan Whitford, for her support, as well as Chris Scott, friend and editor, who read and commented on the manuscript with insight and skill. I would also like to thank Joy Gugeler, my excellent editor at Beach Holme, for helping to whip the final version into shape. And finally, a special thanks to Faith for her generosity and acute observations on the manuscript, and to Elliot for just being Elliot.